"The Deep End Gang"

Peggy Dymond "Leavey"

Napoleon Publishing

Toronto, Ontario, Canada

Cover art: Christopher Chuckry

Published by Napoleon Publishing
Toronto, Ontario, Canada

Le Conseil des Arts du Canada DEPUIS 1957 | The Canada Council for the Arts SINCE 1957

Napoleon Publishing gratefully acknowledges the support of the Canada Council for our publishing program

We acknowledge the support of the Government of Ontario through the Ontario Media Development Corporation's Ontario Book Initiative

Printed in Canada

07 06 05 04 03   5 4 3

National Library of Canada Cataloguing in Publication Data

Leavey, Peggy Dymond, date-
    The deep end gang / Peggy Dymond Leavey

ISBN 0-929141-89-X

I. Title.

PS8573.E2358D43 2003   jC813'.54   C2002-906128-8
PZ7

For Mary, Sheila, Jennifer & John,
who shared my happy, nomadic childhood

One

I knew the first time I saw the house across the street, the day we moved here from Winnipeg, that there was something strange about it. It just didn't seem to fit in. I'm usually the one in the Jessup family who notices these things. The others say I have an overactive imagination, but I ask you: What's a spooky old house with a yard full of weeds doing in the middle of a modern subdivision?

*　　*　　*

Everyone knew we weren't going to live in Winnipeg forever, that someday, usually within two or three years of arriving, we'd be leaving again. So why was my sister Susan making such a big noise about it?

Our old friends in Winnipeg would get along just fine without us, the way they had before we arrived. And we'd make new friends in Ontario.

We always did.

But Susan was acting really weird this time, sniffling in the back seat of the van as we pulled away from the house on Waterloo Street, hauling the camper behind us.

"Hey, Susan," I cried, spotting a couple of my sister's friends coming out of the variety store at the top of our street. "There's Brittany and Rebecca."

"Yo, Britt!" I yelled, my head out the window. "We're leaving!"

Brittany's face wore a bewildered expression, and Susan didn't even bother to look.

When we turned the corner for the last time, my friend Nathan was exactly where he said he'd be—waiting out in front of his place, waving goodbye with both arms.

Nathan had said he wished it were his family that was moving; I'd made it sound like such an adventure. "We'll be going down through the States, driving through North Dakota, Minnesota, Wisconsin and Michigan before we get back to Canada," I told him. It was practically the same route we'd taken two years before, but in the other direction.

My friend had watched with envy as we packed the van, making use of every inch of cargo space for the journey. There was a plastic tote or a hanging bag for everything—the supply of maps, books, magazines, cassette tapes, travel games, pens and pads of paper. The Jessups had gotten very good at packing.

"Okay, folks. We're on our way," Dad announced as we sailed down the ramp and out onto the highway. "Branch, Ontario, here we come!"

Susan pulled her cap down over her eyes and folded her arms across her chest. I think she planned to stay like that all the way to Ontario.

In the past, my sister and I had both looked forward to moving again. What would the new house be like? Would there be kids our age living next door, cool things to do in the new neighbourhood? But that day last April when Dad had come home and said he was posted back to Ontario, Susan had erupted like a volcano, surprising us all. There was no way she was going!

"What about my friends?" she wailed. "I can't leave them. You can't ask me to!" She would stay in Winnipeg, live at Rebecca's, if she had to.

"You can always make new friends," I told her, in my most mature tone.

Susan said she didn't expect a boy to understand. "You're such a *child*," she sneered, with a toss of her red hair. Actually, I'm twelve and a half, barely two years younger than she is. "Of course, *you're* glad to be going," my sister snorted, "after all the lies you've told here."

I was crushed! I didn't tell lies! I just exaggerated

a little. It was nothing more than a habit.

Come to think of it, though, I'd had a couple of close calls. Like the time I said Lulu, our Labrador retriever, was from the same litter as the dog belonging to the American president—at least, the man who had been president when we got Lulu. I nearly got caught with that story.

Susan and her friend Rebecca were out in our driveway one Saturday in March, grooming the dog. I was collecting the chocolate-coloured clumps of hair before the wind caught them and blew them across the snow to the neighbours. Lulu's big brown eyes were rolled back in her head, in ecstasy. She loves any kind of attention.

"Is it true your dog is from the same litter as President Clinton's?" Rebecca asked, pulling the comb through the hair on the dog's back.

"As far as we know," Susan said, without even a sideways glance at me. "You can see how much she looks like the Clintons' dog."

The truth was, the breeder had told us that was *his* theory for why everyone seemed to want this type of dog lately. I was truly amazed that my sister had covered for me like that. I was filled with love and respect for her at that moment.

Love and respect was not what Susan was feeling when she pinned me to my locker at school a few days later. "Don't you ever do that again!" she threatened, green eyes all squeezed up, mean-looking.

"Do what?" I stammered.

"How could you tell everyone that we used to live in a packing case?" she demanded.

"But we did!" I tried to wriggle free of the iron grip she had on the neck of my T-shirt. "Just ask Mom."

"Oh, Martin, a storage shed, not a packing case!" Mom laughed out loud when I asked her for the true story that day after school. "Temporary quarters. And it was just your dad and me. We were newlyweds, and when he arrived at the base where he'd been posted, with a wife, he couldn't stay in barracks."

"But don't you remember you told us the place was so small there was no room for a Christmas tree, even?" I pleaded. "That you got a little one anyway and set it on the kitchen table?" I'd always thought that story illustrated how easily my parents adapted to new surroundings. Dad had attached a rope and pulley to the tree, and when they needed to use the table for meals, they were able to pull the Christmas tree, fully decorated, up to the ceiling, out of the way.

"That's true," Mom concurred. "But it had been a storage shed. And we were only there a few weeks, just until they found a house for us on the base."

"I liked the story better my way," I mumbled.

"Get your facts straight, Martin," Susan hissed, "before you go spreading them around. I don't want everyone, especially my teachers, thinking my brother is a liar. Even if he is!"

My story about the packing case had developed when our sixth grade was doing a study on habitats, and we'd got talking about unusual homes. There was one guy somewhere who lived in a house made out of aluminum cans, and a family in Vermont whose house was buried in the side of a hill. I considered that I'd lived in a few unusual homes myself. From there, the story just sort of snowballed.

As a result of this incident, my sister decided to get to the bottom of what she saw as my problem with the truth. We were both in the kitchen making our supper one night later that week, our parents having gone out to dinner and a movie.

"So, why do you do it, Martin?" Susan asked. "Why do you make up fantastic stories like that?"

"I don't know," I shrugged. I was shaping meatballs for the frying pan from a blob of ground beef.

Susan set the jar of spaghetti sauce down on the counter and turned to face me. "Do you tell these lies so people will like you?"

"I don't think so," I said. "Maybe."

"Why can't you just be yourself? Don't you think just being you is good enough?"

"I don't know," I admitted, puzzled now

myself. "I never thought about why I do it."

"Like, don't you think Lulu's a great dog," Susan badgered, "without you giving her some fake relatives?"

"It's not like that," I insisted. "Sure, she's a great dog. I just thought my story made her a more interesting dog."

"You know, that's really sad, Martin. I think you're pathetic!" Susan lifted the lid off the pot on the stove. "There, the water's ready. Dump the pasta in and watch it doesn't boil over." She left the kitchen, shaking her head.

My sister gives up on me rather easily. But what she said started me thinking. Was I afraid to be just plain, ordinary Martin Jessup—not especially good at anything, unremarkable, easy to forget? Maybe Susan was right. Maybe I *was* pathetic.

Two

We left Winnipeg on the last day of June and arrived in Branch, Ontario, five days later. We had stretched our moving trip into a mini-vacation, taking the long way around to our new home.

As we drove through the town for the first time, Susan, coming out from under her cap and sunglasses, scanned both sides of the main street, looking for shops with recognizable names.

Branch is pretty small compared to Winnipeg. According to Nathan, that was the only drawback to this move. "There's nothing to do in small towns," he'd warned me. "Nothing ever happens there."

The moving van had followed a more direct route east and was long gone by the time we pulled into the driveway of our house on Birch Boulevard, and Dad and I unhooked the camper. We unlocked the front door of our new home to face a barricade of cardboard boxes.

"Why can't these people ever get it right?" Mom

fumed. "You'd think when everything was clearly labelled, they'd know which room was which."

She had that look that meant she was ready to tear her red hair out by the handful when Dad stepped in with a solution. "I vote we go find a pizza before we even think about unpacking," he said. "We're all hungry. Let's eat first and then come back and tackle this, one box at a time."

Mom backed away slowly from the wall of cartons, looking doubtful. "We'll need to find the box with the bedding in it first, Ray, and the lamps."

Flipping a wall switch, Dad showed her that we could do without lamps for a while.

"They have a pizza parlour here?" I asked, afraid my parents were getting side-tracked.

"I didn't see a Roma's," Susan scoffed, pointing her freckled nose skyward.

"That's because Roma owned the Winnipeg place herself," explained Dad. "But I had a pretty fair pizza at Nico's when I was here house-hunting. So, back in the van, everyone. We're hitting the main drag." He was really trying hard to sell us on this place.

It was dark by the time we turned in again at Birch Gardens, our subdivision on the outskirts of Branch. Mom was relieved to find that the movers had followed instructions and at least set up the beds in the three bedrooms on the second floor. Since it was a warm night, we really didn't have to find the box with the sheets or blankets anyway.

The next morning, after we had cleared a path through the packing cartons and found the back door, I stepped out onto a sun-splashed deck and surveyed my new surroundings.

Below the deck was a wide, green lawn with birch saplings planted here and there, no doubt giving the subdivision its name. Beyond was a grassy gully that ran between the backyards of the houses on our street and those on the next. There were definite signs of kids living over there—swing sets and bicycles among the usual gas barbecues and patio furniture.

A tall hedge of cedars hid our neighbours to the west. We weren't so lucky on the other side. That house, which was an exact copy of ours—country-style, two storeys, slate grey siding, white trimmed porch and shutters—was only about a car width from ours.

Lulu was prancing excitedly at the sight of me, so I clipped on her leash, and we walked together around to the front yard. I wanted to get a closer look at the strange house I'd seen across the street.

The dog and I crossed Birch Boulevard to the twin pillars of yellow brick that guarded the entrance to the property. An overgrown driveway curved through the trees and made a loop in front of the house. The house itself was three storeys high with a steep roof sheathed in tin. Several of the window shutters, maroon paint flaking off, were hanging by only one hinge. I decided my first impression had been right. There definitely was something weird about an old house like that in the middle of a modern subdivision.

A chain had come unhooked from one of the pillars and lay in the driveway, the metal sign it used to carry face down in the dried mud. Picking up the chain, I swung the sign over to read, "Trespassers will be prosecuted." By the neglected appearance of the property, I seriously doubted that.

As Lulu and I crossed back to our side of the street and cut between our house and the next, I noticed someone sitting on the porch next door. "Morning," I called out.

A bald head turned slowly, and a man's face scowled at us over the railing. He didn't speak.

Oh well, I thought, maybe he's concerned about the dog. "We'll be keeping Lulu tied," I promised, but the man had already turned away. It didn't look as if there were any kids living in his house anyway.

I was bound to make some friends by the time school started. That's all I wanted—some familiar faces on my first day. I'm always starting a new school. And it isn't always in September. I've been to so many different schools that I've lost count. Susan says she's been to six.

That's just the way it is with the armed forces. Mom tells us she knew when she married Dad that she wouldn't be putting down roots until his career in the military was over. My father was originally from New Brunswick. Susan was born in Barrie, Ontario, and I arrived while they were living in Edmonton, Alberta. But home was wherever we were living when anyone asked.

Three

We didn't have long to wait that first morning before visitors showed up at the back door. The two kids from the house across the gully, the one with the basketball hoop on the back of the garage, told us they had watched the moving van unload days before we arrived. They'd been waiting ever since for signs of life at our house.

Granger and Crystal Fletcher were both tall and skinny, with white-blonde hair, almost invisible lashes, and clear, light blue eyes. The boy had the worst case of poison ivy I'd ever seen. He was almost a year younger than I was, and a full head taller, but because I was born at the first of the year and Granger at the end of it, we were both going into Grade Seven. Granger's sister was the same age as Susan.

Their mother followed them over a little while later. Another tall, pale figure, she rapped on the back door and apologized for her family's intrusion. "They wanted to come over the minute you arrived," she smiled, "but I made them wait till you'd had a good night's sleep, at least."

Mrs. Fletcher had brought with her a basket of warm carrot muffins, but she waved off Mom's invitation to stay for coffee. Mom hadn't actually found the coffee maker yet, anyway. She and Dad had dunked a tea bag between them at breakfast.

"If my two are going to hang around, you put them both to work," Mrs. Fletcher advised as she backed out the door again. I moved in on the basket of muffins.

Having two extra pairs of hands did speed up the unpacking, especially once Dad developed a system where he found the box Mom needed, Granger and I took it in to her, and she and the two girls put its contents where they thought best.

"You guys sure must move around a lot," Granger remarked, carrying a small table we'd unearthed into what would be the den. "I counted eleven movers' stickers stuck to the bottom of this table."

By noon hour, Granger's poison ivy was starting to drive him crazy, and he went home to put some more lotion on it. He did not come back after lunch. Since Crystal had to go to her swimming lesson, Susan shut herself in her room for the afternoon, leaving me to empty the boxes marked "Martin's Stuff" in mine.

It was smaller than the bedroom I'd had in

Winnipeg, but this one had one interesting possibility: its window opened out onto the almost flat roof of the front porch—the perfect vantage point from which to observe the neighbourhood.

I decided to check it out and, swinging the window wide, I put one foot out onto the roof. I was immediately disappointed to discover that the black roofing material was sticky from the heat of the sun. I'd have to wait till later in the day when it cooled down to walk on it.

On the other side of the road was that spooky yellow house. Its tall, narrow windows were set in three-sided bays that rose to the steep, tin roof. The tin was stamped with a pattern that looked to me like giant fish scales. Totally weird.

It was obvious that no one lived in the house, no one who owned a lawn mower, anyway. The grass in the yard was a foot high. There were no cars in the driveway, no chairs on the long side verandah behind the torn and rusted screens, no sign of life anywhere. Tall pine trees grew on three sides of the property and cast dark shadows over the house and yard, even at midday. There were newer houses on both sides of it, making it look like something time forgot.

"What a fine old place that must have been," Mom remarked, coming into the room with a hamper full of shoes and sneakers and joining me at the window. "Someone's ancestral home, I'll bet."

"I don't think there's anyone living there now," I said. "Unless it's someone's ghost."

Mom unloaded some of the sneakers onto the floor of my closet and looked around. "So, what do you think, Martin? This is a pretty nice room, isn't it?"

"Sure, it's fine, Mom."

"You'll like it here, son." She patted my head with its close-cropped summer hair cut. Her voice was soft. "You've always made friends easily, adjusted well."

"Susan will get used to it too," I pointed out.

"Sure she will," Mom agreed. "She's just at the age now when her friendships are very intense, so leaving them is harder." She turned in the doorway and looked back towards me. "I think I have a pair of curtains somewhere that will fit that window."

*　　*　　*

It didn't take me long to discover that the house across the street wasn't the only thing about this neighbourhood that was weird. There was also something peculiar about the bald guy who lived next door. Every day since we'd arrived, I'd seen him sitting on his porch in exactly the same spot. And he stayed there all day, never moving.

He was very overweight and always dressed in

black. With his many chins, his pouchy face and hairless head, his massive shoulders that slouched forward as he sat, he reminded me of a toad—if toads were heavy smokers. It was creepy. It wasn't that the man was watching us; he never even seemed to turn his head. But the way I saw it, he had to be watching something.

As usual, Mom hung her signs on the front and back doors of the new house, indicating that ours was a smoke-free home. She was adamant about this, and I would not have been surprised if she'd informed our silent neighbour that he was infringing on our right to clean air.

One morning, however, I was up a little earlier than usual, and I saw an athletic-looking man, dressed in white jeans and T-shirt, wheel our neighbour out of the house and into his favourite position on the porch. I was sure it was that wheelchair that kept Mom from voicing her objection to the smoke that often drifted over to our porch.

I began to notice that the white-garbed attendant would reappear in the late afternoon to take the man back into the house. Then, after a little while, the attendant would drive away again in a shiny red Corvette that had been parked at the curb. A well-paid attendant. Very interesting, I thought.

My sister seemed determined to find nothing

in this new place that interested her. "So, what kind of a name is 'Branch', anyway?" she demanded in one of her breakfast moods on Monday morning.

Dad looked up from his corn flakes. "I believe it's called that because this is where the river branches," he said, wiping milk off his chin.

"Now, there's a summer project for the two of you." Mom seized on the subject with enthusiasm. She has always been big on projects. "Why not research the origin of the name of our new home?"

I looked across the table at Susan. She rolled her eyes at the ceiling.

Dad, already dressed in his army uniform, poured coffee into his travel mug. It was his first day back at work. "There's the Upper Danby River and the Lower Danby," he said thoughtfully. "The town is built right at the place where they fork."

"So why not call it Fork?" I queried. This got a snort from Susan.

Four

I took it as a sign that Susan might be coming around when she agreed to go swimming at the pool with Crystal on Wednesday morning. Mom, who is a registered practical nurse and never has any trouble finding work, had an interview with the director of nursing at the hospital. Just as I was about to make plans for my own day, Susan asked me to keep Granger company.

"He can't go swimming on account of the poison ivy," she explained, wrinkling her nose. "And since his summer is pretty much ruined anyhow, he's coming over. Okay?" She made it sound as if I could only add to his misery.

So, there was Granger at the back door, his poison ivy all painted with white stuff, making it even more obvious. "Your sister said maybe I could keep you company," he suggested mournfully. "But I'll bet you wanted to go to the pool too."

"No, that's okay," I said, feeling sorry for him. So far, he seemed like the kind of kid who thought that he had to carry the weight of the world's problems around on his skinny shoulders. Besides, who else was I going to hang out with?

"What do you want to do, then?" he asked, as if I'd invited him over.

"Well, maybe we could kick the soccer ball around a bit?"

"Can't," said Granger. "I'm not supposed to get sweaty. Do you want to watch TV?"

"In the daytime? Anyway, we're waiting for the cable company to come and hook us up."

In the end, we decided to take Lulu for a walk. I was anxious to explore the town beyond Birch Gardens anyway, and walking a dog is always a good excuse. We were just attaching Lulu's leash at the foot of the back steps when a girl dressed in khaki shorts and a bright red T-shirt strode through an opening in the cedars to the west and marched towards us. She was stockily built, with shoulder-length, dark brown hair scraped back from her forehead by a circular comb. It gave her flushed, round face a look of constant surprise.

"Oh, here's Holly," said Granger, sounding relieved. "Have you met her yet?"

"Welcome to Branch and to Birch Gardens," Holly said, as if she were a greeter at Wal-Mart. "I'm Holly Valentine, and I live next door. I'd have been over before, but I had to go to the orthodontist in the city." She gave an exaggerated smile to reveal the braces on her teeth. "I see you've met the Fletchers." Holly peered closely into Granger's swollen face and asked, "Is that stuff itchy?"

"Pretty much," said Granger.

"I remember you had it before, didn't you?"

"Nearly every year," nodded Granger, sadly.

Holly stroked Lulu's head between the ears. "Nice dog," she remarked. "So what are you guys doing, anyway?"

"Not much," I admitted. "Trying not to sweat, for Granger's sake."

"We were just going to walk the dog," said Granger. "I'm going to show Martin around a bit."

"Then I'll go with you," decided Holly. She didn't wait to be invited.

Lulu, accompanied by the three of us, headed west on Birch Boulevard towards the highway. "Martin's from Winnipeg," Granger volunteered, as we followed the dog. "His dad's in the military."

"He's got a long drive to work, then," Holly observed. "How come you don't live out on the base? They've got their own school there and everything."

"We've lived in PMQs before," I explained. "That's what they call the houses on the base. But when Dad found a place we could rent here in Birch Gardens, he jumped at it."

"The Jessups move all the time," said Granger sorrowfully.

"What's all the time?" Holly asked.

"Every couple of years."

"Really?" Holly seemed surprised. "Do you like moving that much?"

"Sure. It doesn't bother me," I said. "It's something we've always done."

We had turned onto the busy Townline Road, where we could walk side by side along its edge. Holly switched places with me so that I could keep Lulu further from the traffic.

"I've never moved," Granger grumbled.

"Me neither," said Holly. "I don't think I'd want to."

"Oh, it's not so bad," I said. "When you're little, you don't even think about it. It's kind of an adventure, something to look forward to."

"Does that mean someday you'll have to move away from here?" Granger asked.

"Practically guaranteed," I told him.

"Bummer," said Granger.

We had been walking about twenty minutes when we crossed a cement bridge over the place where the Upper and Lower Danby met, where it rushed over stones and boulders to tumble into Lizzy Lake. East of the bridge we found ourselves in the downtown part of Branch. The main street stretched for about a kilometre, a block above the shore of the lake. There was a small marina with two docks extending out into the water, where a few pleasure boats were moored, and a section of sand reserved for a public beach.

"A lake right in town is pretty cool," I observed. Families were already unloading chairs and beach toys and lugging coolers from their cars in the gravel parking lot. "You guys swim here often?"

"It gets pretty crowded," said Holly. Lawn chairs and bright umbrellas sprouted from the sandy shore.

"We mostly go to the indoor pool," Granger explained. "On account of that's where we take lessons. I was taking diving lessons until I got poison ivy."

"Well, you'll be able to go back when you're better, won't you?" I asked.

"I guess," said Granger, but he didn't sound very happy about it. It seemed to me that Granger's mood was gloomy most of the time. Maybe it was all the itching.

The buildings on Main Street in Branch included the post office, the bank, the library and the firehall. Halfway down the street was a small park where lush grass ran to the edge of the water. Since that seemed to be the place Lulu wanted to visit, we followed. There was a bandshell in the middle of the park and some well-used playground equipment. Tying the dog to one of the steel uprights, the three of us sat on the swings and dangled for a while, kicking at the sand under our sneakers and watching a hairy man in a muscle shirt apply paint the colour of butter to the railing around the bandshell.

"I guess you guys have known each other a long time," I remarked.

"All our lives, practically," agreed Holly.

"I've never known anyone for my whole life," I admitted. "Except for my family, of course."

"We used to call ourselves the Dynamic Duo," said Granger with a sly look at Holly.

I let the chain on my swing unwind. It was only a matter of time before these two would start reminding each other of school trips and other fun times that weren't part of my memory. I knew the routine.

"Come on," I said, "let's go." Lulu had tired of sniffing out the park, anyway.

I bought a box of fries from the chip wagon parked on the empty lot at the corner, and we shared the greasy food as we strolled up to the next block. Here, separated by a chain link fence and a sea of concrete, were the school and the community centre that housed the pool and arena. A caretaker was mowing the margin of grass at the front of the school, and he raised a hand in greeting when we stopped to take a look.

"Hi, Fred," Holly called.

Holly, too, I learned, would be going into Grade Seven at the school in the fall. Whether or not the three of us would be in the same class remained to be seen. I hoped we would be. It's always better going into a new school if you already know a few of your classmates. Susan and Crystal were going to be bussed to the big high school out of town. I didn't know if my sister would ever get over her disappointment at not going to Kelvin in Winnipeg.

"So, that's it," declared Holly as we left the schoolyard and turned homeward again. "There's a mall out on the highway, but that's it for beautiful, downtown Branch."

"It's small," I agreed. "But we've lived in small towns before."

"Not much happening, compared to Winnipeg," remarked Granger. He had asked to hold Lulu's leash on the way back.

There was a big smiley face sign on the outskirts of town, and we stopped there to rest for a few moments. The sign invited us to "pay another visit to Branch, the town with 2500 friendly folks."

The Jessup family already knew the Fletchers and the Valentines were friendly. Holly's parents had come over the night before, and Mr. Valentine had helped Dad to lug our metal patio furniture up onto the back deck. We'd all stayed out there till long after dark. The last thing I heard before turning in myself was Mr. Valentine teasing Dad about bringing the mosquitoes from Winnipeg.

"I guess you've met Mr. Deitz by now," Holly observed.

When I looked puzzled, she explained. "Sam Deitz, the man on the other side of your house."

"I didn't know that was his name," I admitted. "He doesn't say much, does he? I guess he's not one of the friendly folk your sign here brags about."

"You got that right," Granger agreed with a grim look. "That guy's totally weird."

I nodded. "I figured as much."

Holly bristled. "That's not a very nice thing to say, Granger. The man's in a wheelchair, after all."

"The wheelchair has nothing to do with it," Granger defended himself. "The guy's unfriendly. Even my mother said so. He doesn't want to be bothered with any of us."

Lulu, eager to investigate the place every other dog in town had visited, had managed to wind her leash around the signpost as well as Granger's legs. He was trying to extricate himself and was getting pretty agitated.

"Mr. Deitz just wants to be left alone," Holly explained calmly. She commandeered the dog's leash, and circling Granger and the post, she separated them from each other with no problem. "My dad says he's entitled to his privacy."

"People who want that much privacy sometimes have something to hide," I suggested.

Five

In spite of the fries, my stomach was rumbling when we reached the subdivision again at noon hour. I let Lulu circle our yard before putting her back on her rope. Then, unwinding the hose from the side of the house, I filled her water bowl to overflowing, the dog lapping at the cool liquid almost before it hit the dish.

"See you guys this afternoon, then?" I said, as the other two turned to leave.

"Come over whenever you're ready," Holly invited.

Since no one was home at my house, I made myself a generous peanut butter and jam sandwich and took it out on the back deck to eat. I spent the next half-hour picking raspberry seeds out of my teeth and waiting for Granger to show up again. When he didn't, I made my way through the hedge to find Holly myself.

"She's out the back, dear." Mrs. Valentine came to the door, a smile crinkling the corners of the same sharp brown eyes as Holly had. "Just go through those trees out there. You'll find her." And find her I did, but in the most unexpected place.

My new friend was sitting in a plastic lawn chair, in the deep end of an old, empty swimming pool at the back of the Valentines' property. She had her feet up on a second chair, her nose buried in a book.

"Hey, this is cool," I remarked, looking down into the large rectangle of flaking grey cement. "How come there's no water in it?"

"This is my father's project," Holly said, closing her book and looking up at me. Her face was dappled in leaf shadows.

"You mean he built this? It looks kind of old." I went to the other end and descended the pie-shaped, cement steps in one corner. About halfway down, the floor of the pool sloped quickly towards the deep end before levelling out again.

"No, he didn't build it," Holly explained. She removed her feet from the other chair. "It was here before the subdivision, even."

"Isn't there supposed to be water in it?"

"There was once, I guess. Now it leaks pretty badly. This is the pool from the old Govier estate. Dad wouldn't let the contractor bulldoze it in when he had the house built. One of these days he's going to restore it, he says. Mom says if we're going to have a swimming pool, it won't be this one. She calls it an eyesore."

"So, what's the Govier estate?" I asked, lowering myself, uninvited, into the other chair.

"Didn't you see that old house across the street? That's the Govier place. They used to own all this land, the whole subdivision. My dad says they had a tennis court where your house is."

"No kidding? I wish they'd left that."

"I guess Dad had to fight to keep this, had to buy an extra lot. I think I'll be sorry if he ever gets around to filling it with water. It's been my favourite place for a long time. They can't see me here from the house, on account of the trees. Dad used to keep it covered to keep the rain water out, and because they were afraid I'd fall in when I was little. Now they know that whenever I want some peace and quiet, this is where I'll be."

"Do you want me to leave?" I asked, eyeing the book in her lap.

"No, that's okay. My friends are welcome." She stood and stretched freckled arms above her head. "The Grange always knows where to find me. I'm sort of a bookworm," she added, sounding apologetic about it.

I understood. "No problem. We're all bookworms at my house. The movers always complain about all the heavy boxes of books we have."

The deep end of the pool, except where Holly had swept an area clear for her chairs and a low, plastic table with three legs, was littered with sticks and a thick layer of damp leaves.

Holly watched as I poked at the debris with a stick I'd picked up. "I found an old rubber bathing cap buried under the leaves down here one time," she said. "It was red, and the rubber pulled apart in my hands. It must have been here for years and years. It made me wonder who might have lost it."

"Awesome," I said. "Do you think the Goviers had pool parties?" That made Holly laugh. Maybe she was imagining, as I was, scenes of rowdy parties I'd seen in old movies, where the people danced the Charleston till they toppled, one by one, into the swimming pool.

"There's been a notice in the paper for weeks now," Holly was saying. "The Govier house is going to be sold for back taxes. Dad thinks someone will likely tear it down to make way for more new homes."

"I was going to ask you what the story was on that place," I said. "It *is* kind of creepy-looking."

"I know," said Holly. "It's been deserted for a long time."

We heard someone calling from the backyard. It was Granger. "Are you out here, Holly?" he called. He came to the edge and gazed down at us. "Thought I'd find you here." Granger stood there for a moment, a mournful expression on his face. "I guess you don't have enough chairs," he decided.

"Come on down," Holly invited. "I'll get another chair. I'm going up for a cold drink anyway. I'll bring us all one. Lemonade okay?"

"It's not sour, is it?" Granger asked.

After Holly had left for the house, Granger slumped in the chair she had vacated, dabbing gingerly at the poison ivy blisters on his arms with a tissue.

"Holly's cool," I remarked. "I mean, for a girl."

Granger looked surprised. "She's been my friend since kindergarten," he said. "I don't think of her as a girl. The only other kids on this street are really little." He sighed and tucked the tissue back into the pocket of his shorts. "I guess you've noticed Holly's sort of bossy? She's the smartest one in our class too. My dad keeps hoping I'll catch some of her smarts. So far, it hasn't happened."

It was Holly who came up with the idea that afternoon of the three of us forming a club. "Since we all live so close and seem to get along with each other," she reasoned. "What do you think? This could be our regular meeting place, right here in the pool. We could call ourselves The Three Musketeers or something."

"Right," agreed Granger, eagerly, "after the chocolate bar."

"It's not after the chocolate bar, Grange," Holly pointed out patiently. "It's after the book."

"What about something more original?" was my suggestion. "How about the Deep End Gang?"

"Excellent!" cried Holly. "I like that."

"How come I never come up with ideas like that?" Granger grumbled.

"I have a pretty good imagination," I admitted. "In fact, in certain circles I have a reputation for it." When it looked as if they might want to know more about this facet of my personality, I continued. "My sister Susan says I make up stories to impress people, to get them to like me. Pretty pathetic, right?"

"We like you." Granger scratched at the back of his neck. "Have you done it to us yet?"

"No," I realized. "Everything I've told you is the plain truth."

Holly looked thoughtful. "Do you think you try to impress people because you're always having to find new friends?" she suggested. "Since you're always moving?"

"Could be, I guess."

Something suddenly dawned on Granger. "Since you guys have to move so much, that must mean you have to go to a different school every time, right?"

"Right," I agreed.

"If I had to walk into a school where no one knew me, I'd throw up," Granger stated. "That's what I do when I get upset. All the time."

"He does, too," Holly confirmed.

"Oh, it's not that bad," I told them. "The teacher usually makes a big thing about introducing you to the class. It makes you kind of special, for a while. Everyone hangs around you, wanting to know where you came from, all that kind of stuff. You're the centre of attention. For a while."

The others nodded as if they understood, but I knew they couldn't. Being the new kid was something you had to experience to appreciate.

The air was cool in the bottom of the old swimming pool, and our voices echoed off the walls above our heads. The windbreak of mature trees that surrounded the pool provided a canopy to shade us from the afternoon sun. Every once in a while another leaf fluttered down to add to the pungent carpet at our feet.

"It's all in the way you look at things," declared Holly finally, draining her glass of pink lemonade. "Having a vivid imagination can be a good thing. You know, my dad says that in a club everyone contributes what they're best at, their strong points. Your strength, Martin, is your excellent imagination." She was crunching on ice cubes now. "Mine is my organizational skill."

"And your brains," Granger added. Then we both looked at him. You could tell he was wondering what we thought were his strengths.

"Yours is your loyalty, Grange," Holly jumped

in quickly. "Absolutely."

"I was going to say your friendliness," I offered him. "You were the first person here to want to be my friend."

"Well, Holly wasn't exactly home," Granger allowed.

"That's true," said Holly. "But I'd bought a new book while I was away, and when I got home I stayed down here till I'd finished it. *Then* I went over."

Six

We had been in Branch for two weeks, and most of the time my sister Susan stayed in her room with the door shut. When she did emerge, she walked around the house like a zombie. She said she wasn't interested in meeting any of Crystal Fletcher's other friends, and she only saw Crystal because Mom insisted she get out of the house once in a while.

Then one day, a letter came from her old friend Rebecca, inviting Susan to go back to Winnipeg to spend next Christmas with her family. Susan immediately came to life. "Can I, Mom? Daddy? Please?"

Our parents were on their hands and knees, laying a runner of carpet in the upstairs hallway, backing their way towards the stairs.

"Christmas is a long way off," said Mom over her shoulder, sounding cautious.

"And so's Winnipeg," declared Dad. He grabbed the bannister and got to his feet. "How are you going to get there?"

"I'll go by bus. I still have my babysitting money in the bank. I already found out how much it would cost. I can pay for my own ticket."

I saw the look Mom and Dad exchanged. I knew they were thinking that it was not a good sign that Susan had already investigated the cost of a ticket.

"We'll have to think about it," said Mom. From years of experience, Susan and I both knew that was not necessarily a positive response.

"Well!" Susan huffed. "I don't know what you expect me to do around this place!"

"I have an idea," Mom offered, sitting back on her heels. "I noticed that movie you thought you'd missed in Winnipeg is showing here already. Why don't you and your brother go to the show?"

"Mother, please!"

"Want to, Susan?" I asked from my position on the stairs, where I was in charge of tape measures and cutting tools.

"I don't plan on being seen at the show with my brother, after dark," my sister retorted.

I hadn't heard that excuse before. "But it isn't dark," I reminded her.

"No, but it will be by the time the show's out," Susan said, and she flounced past us, up to her room.

So it was the Deep End Gang who went to the movies that evening. Holly and Granger were better company anyhow. Mom and Dad dropped us off on their way to the home improvement centre, and Holly's mother said she would pick us up after the show.

The movie was okay, but the air conditioning was cranked so high that we shivered all the way through it.

Afterwards, the three of us stood out in front of the theatre waiting for Mrs. Valentine. By nine-forty, everyone else had wandered off down the street or caught their rides home, and still Holly's mother hadn't shown up. Even at that hour the night air was still hot, heavy with flying insects.

The theatre staff left, and finally the manager came out of the building and locked the door. He eyed us with grown-up suspicion. "You kids got skateboards?"

"No, sir. We were at the show."

"Well, I don't want you hanging around here anyway," he growled.

"We're waiting for our ride, sir," I told him. He frowned, as if he didn't believe me, but then he left us alone.

"This is so not-like-Mom," Holly declared, stepping out to the curb for the hundredth time and checking the street in both directions.

"Think we'd better walk?" I suggested.

Holly wasn't sure. "Mom said she'd come."

"Maybe she forgot," Granger intoned, Eeyore-like.

"No, she wouldn't forget," said Holly, assuredly. "She probably just had company drop by, or something." She looked first at Granger, then at me. "Well, maybe we should walk. You okay with that, Grange?"

"I guess," he grumbled, swatting at mosquitoes.

"Come on, then," Holly decided. "We can take the shortcut."

A block up, we turned off the main street and followed a street lined with houses to the outskirts of town. There was a plaza here with eight or ten shops and offices. Holly led us through the video store parking lot to an opening in the chain-link fence that separated the back of the plaza and a wooded area. We followed a narrow, worn path along the edge of the trees.

"This eventually comes out at Townline Road," Holly informed us. She was in front, and Granger was stumbling along behind me. It was dark now, and the only light came from back of the plaza. The stench from an overflowing dumpster permeated the air.

"I'm not supposed to take this shortcut," Granger announced suddenly.

At that, Holly stopped so quickly that I walked into her. "Oh, my gawd! That's right!" She clapped her hand over her mouth. "This is exactly where it happened, isn't it?"

"On the other side of the fence," groaned Granger.

"Don't stop. Keep walking! Geez, Holly," he whined, "why didn't your mother come and get us?"

I took my eyes off the path long enough to see that we were directly behind the drive-through for the Dairy Dipt. Everything seemed okay to me, except for the smell. We could hear the crackling tones of the girl on the speaker, telling the customer that his bill came to five dollars and thirty cents, and to "please drive ahead."

"What happened?" I asked. "What are you talking about?"

"Come on," barked Holly. "I'll tell you later. We've got to hurry."

We were walking up the back of one another's heels by the time we emerged from the underbrush at the lights of Townline Road, the main thoroughfare to our subdivision. Now we were able to walk on the grassy shoulder, where the passing traffic provided some movement of the stifling air. "Okay, now tell me," I demanded.

"Well, it happened like this," Holly began, dramatically. "One night, a man who owned one of the businesses in the plaza was murdered." In spite of the heat, goose bumps sprang out on my arms and legs. "It happened right there at the back door to his business. The other employees had all left, and he was just locking up. He had the day's receipts with him and was about to cross the parking lot and get into his car."

"But," Granger took up the story, "he never got there! Next day, there were signs of a struggle, but all they found were his reading glasses in the long grass next to the fence."

"Where was his body found?" I asked.

"It wasn't," replied Holly. "That's part of the mystery. No body was ever found. His car was still in the parking lot the next day. His key was still in the back door of the office."

"But if they didn't have a body," I protested, "how do they know he was murdered? Maybe he was kidnapped."

"They thought of that. But no one ever got a ransom note. He just vanished. Never heard from again."

"My dad had this theory that his body was likely dumped into Lizzy Lake," offered Granger. "But the police dragged the lake and didn't find him. Found my sister's old bicycle, though."

We walked in silence for a few minutes, the traffic rushing past us. "Here's Mom now," cried Holly as a van pulled onto the shoulder ahead of us and stopped.

The door of the van slid open, and we climbed in. "Sorry, kids," Mrs. Valentine apologized. "I got in the van to come get you and realized I was almost out of gas. My usual station was closed, so I had to go across town. Then I must have missed you somewhere. Everything okay?"

"Sure, fine," said Holly, throwing a warning look at the two of us sitting behind her. Granger looked more than ever like he'd seen a ghost. A murder, right here in Branch. Who said nothing ever happens in small towns?

*   *   *

Later that night, before I got into bed, I lifted the screen out of my window and stepped out onto the porch roof. The night was alive with the creaking of frogs, and the sky overhead deep with stars, stretching on and on into infinity. A train throbbed in the distance.

I slid down against the side of the house until I was sitting, hugging my knees. From this vantage point I could see all the way back to the lights of Townline Road.

I thought about the story I'd just heard and considered sending an email to Nathan back in Winnipeg, telling him about it. He'd definitely be impressed, might even change his mind about small towns. But I knew I'd probably never send that letter. Unlike Susan, who wrote to Rebecca practically every week, I didn't keep in touch with old friends. Once we moved away, they were history. I was pretty sure they never thought of me again anyway.

The others in my family felt differently. When

I'd arrived home that evening, Mom and Dad had been ecstatic about running into the Meuniers at the home improvement centre. We'd been neighbours when we lived on the base at Petawawa. Their son Jean-Paul was the same age as Susan. My parents had invited the Meuniers over to dinner at the end of the month. The chance to become reacquainted with old military friends was one of the good things about moving, they said. Except in this case, there were no kids my age.

Suddenly, something across the road caught my eye. As I turned my attention towards it, I saw it again. There was a light in the deserted house on the other side of the street!

While I watched, the light behind the curtains moved from one downstairs window to another. After a minute or two, I saw it again on the floor above. Then it went out.

Intrigued, I watched for maybe ten minutes more, my eyes straining into the dark, but I didn't see it again. Obviously, the old Govier house was not deserted after all.

I stepped back in through my window and spied Susan standing in the doorway. "You're not supposed to take that screen out," she bossed. "No wonder the house is full of mosquitoes."

"Come here a sec," I said. "You know that old house across the road? I just saw a light in the window there!"

"So?"

"Well, no one lives there any more. Have *you* ever seen any lights on?"

"I haven't really bothered to look," she replied loftily. "Who cares? Mom says it's for sale. Maybe someone's looking it over before they buy it."

"At night?"

"Well, like I said, who cares?" And without even coming into the room, she headed down the hall for her own.

"Susan, listen." I scurried after her. "I'm going to get a rug or a blanket or something and take it out there, look at stars and stuff. It's really nice out on the roof. Come and try it."

"That'll look totally gross from the street, Martin—a bunch of junk up there. Everyone will know for sure my brother's a nut case." She slammed her door.

I left the screen standing beside the window as I got ready for bed, and I kept checking the house on the other side of the street. Everything now was in darkness. I wished it were already morning. I couldn't wait to share this bit of news with the Deep End Gang.

Seven

W here are you off to so early?" Mom demanded after watching me wolf down my breakfast the next morning.

"Just to see the guys," I replied. My hand was already gripping the knob on the back door.

"It's Saturday," Dad reminded me. "You and I have some chores to do together, haven't we? You were going to help with the new shelves for the garage."

"And doesn't Granger deliver the weekend paper on Saturday mornings?" Mom inquired. She was right, as usual.

It was ten-thirty before I finally got away from them. Granger had already left for Holly's by the time I got to his place. At the Valentines', I found them both sitting in the old swimming pool, comparing battle scars. Granger's poison ivy had left him with some minor scabs on his arms and legs that looked pretty impressive. But Holly had knelt on a nail last May and got an infection in the wound that had resulted in a large, white scar on her right knee. Since she swore it would be permanent, she was definitely the winner.

"Okay, you guys." I interrupted the inspection. "You absolutely are not going to believe this!" They both looked at me expectantly. I half wished I could reveal some huge appendectomy scar for them.

"Last night," I began with a flourish, "I saw lights in the old Govier house."

"Get out!" gasped Holly. "You couldn't have!"

"It's true. I swear." I drew up the third chair to face them.

Granger's mouth had dropped open, and his blue eyes bulged. "You did? But it's deserted."

"Not last night, it wasn't," I crowed.

"This isn't one of those made-up stories you said you liked to tell, is it, Martin?" asked Holly, narrowing her eyes at me. "To impress us?"

"Absolutely not."

"Wow," breathed Granger.

"You sure it wasn't a reflection?" Holly said. "You know, headlights on a car?"

"I know what headlights look like, Holly."

"I mean, if the car was turning off the next street?"

I shook my head. "I watched for a long time," I insisted. "At least an hour."

"Wow," said Granger again. "That's amazing."

"Well, okay, maybe not for a whole hour," I

admitted, remembering I had made a promise to myself to try to control the exaggerating. "But for a long time."

"You know what's really amazing?" asked Holly. "It's that we were all just talking about the murder."

I frowned. "I don't get the connection."

"Well, that's his house, Martin!" Granger exclaimed.

"You mean," I gulped, "the dead guy who was murdered? He lived there?"

"Not exactly," said Holly. "He didn't live there at the time of the murder. He grew up there. It was his family's home. His mother was the last person to live in the house. She's been dead three or four years, at least. You know, it was really sad because after the murder everyone said she kept hoping her son would be found alive." Holly returned to examining her knees. "But he never was."

I thought I understood. "And I bet she died of a broken heart. Right?"

"Nope, it was a stroke," Granger stated flatly. "My mother told me."

"So, about the lights," Holly said, looking up again. "It must mean the power is still on in the house."

"Well, they weren't electric lights that light up a whole room," I explained. "More like moving lights."

"Candlelight or flashlight?" queried Holly.

"How would I know?"

"Candlelight flickers; flashlight is steadier, sort of sweeps around."

"Flashlight then," I decided.

Holly considered that for a moment. "I wonder what could be going on over there," she said.

"And what do you think it means?" Granger ventured in a hollow tone.

"Obviously that someone was in the house," I told him.

"But who?" asked Holly. "That's the question. It can't just be someone who plans to buy the house. They'd turn on the lights."

"Unless the power is off, like you said," Granger suggested.

"So, they'd go in the daytime, if it was," countered Holly. "And you'd see a car in the driveway, at least. This way, it looks very suspicious."

Granger and I both agreed that it did.

"Fellow members, gentlemen." Holly stood up and cleared her throat. "I think this should be the first mission for the Deep End Gang."

"It should?"

"Well, you don't just form a club with no purpose in mind. I'd been wondering what ours could be. This is it! We will find out who is getting into the Govier house and what they're looking for. What do you think?"

"Fine by me," I said. "I was wondering, is there

still furniture and stuff in there, things someone might want to steal?"

Holly nodded. "There must be. Mom said she was interested in having a look around before the sale. There could be antiques or something."

"Don't you think maybe we should tell someone about this?" Granger suggested. "Like the police?"

"Not yet," decided Holly. "Who's going to believe a kid? Anyway, we need more evidence. So, here's the plan." She was taking command, as usual. "I say Martin continues to keep an eye on the house. Okay, Martin? You have the best place to watch from. My room's at the back of the house, and yours is in the wrong block entirely, Grange."

I agreed. "Then what?"

"Report back here to the other members of the Gang if you see anything. Simple enough."

"Right," I nodded. "Then what?"

"Well, if it happens again, we'll have to take action," Holly replied.

Neither Granger nor I had the nerve to ask what action she had in mind.

*   *   *

"Would you have any old rugs or cushions or stuff that I could sit on, out on the porch roof?" I asked Mom as I loaded the supper dishes into the dishwasher that evening.

Mom frowned. "What are people going to think, having someone sitting out on the roof?" She was starting to sound like Susan.

"They won't see me, Mom," I promised. "It's dark when I go out. It's too hot on the roof in the daytime anyway. But at night, it's the most excellent place to stargaze. And I'm inviting all of you out onto my roof for the Perseides meteor shower next month."

"I can hardly wait," muttered Susan.

"Well, just don't start taking things out there and leaving them in full view, or to get wet," Mom advised. But she found me an old mover's pad to sit on.

So I began a nightly vigil of the Govier house. Every night for a week I took up my post on the porch roof and watched while the lights around the neighbourhood went out, one by one.

On Wednesday night, I saw someone in the house west of Govier's looking back at me, his face up close to the glass, and then I saw the drapes sweep quickly over the window. "Sorry, mister," I said, "I wasn't looking at you."

It didn't take long for me to learn that the older couple on the other side of the Goviers turned in every night by nine o'clock. And I noticed too how the light in the upstairs window in the house with the new baby down the block would come on several times, very late.

Although I stayed out on the roof every night until after midnight, I never saw lights in the Govier house again. As my lack of sleep began to catch up with me, I slept in later and later each morning. The other members of the Deep End Gang would be waiting impatiently for my report by the time I arrived at the pool.

"Nothing," I would tell them, yawning. It was hard to keep the disappointment out of my voice.

"Well, there's always tonight," Holly, the optimist, would say.

"Maybe you were imagining it," said Granger.

I just glared at him.

Eight

It had been a long week for the Grange too. Every day, he'd been expecting a visit from his father. He'd warned us, with a happy grin, that we likely wouldn't see much of him once his dad arrived in town. But here it was Saturday already, and Granger was there in the deep end with Holly when I went out back. "Hey," I said, "wasn't this the week that your dad was coming?"

"He sent me a tent instead," mumbled Granger, avoiding my eyes. He was bent over a maple leaf, systematically stripping the veins out of it.

Holly had picked up the broom and busied herself sweeping the floor of the pool, saying nothing. I took the chair beside my friend. I guessed the plan was to wait until Granger was ready to talk about what was bugging him.

"Mom calls the tent a peace offering," he choked, finally. "He was supposed to take me camping."

I felt sorry for him, and I handed him another leaf. He'd really mangled the first one. He gave me back a thin smile. "When are you going to try the tent out?" I asked.

"I don't know." Granger shrugged. "Sometime, I guess."

"What about tonight?" He didn't seem to hear me. "I mean, is it big enough for two?"

"Well, it says on the bag that it's a three-man tent. Why? Do you want to try it out with me?"

"Sure. Why not?" I saw his face brighten. "It would be fun."

"Now, just a minute." Holly set the broom against the wall and stood with her hands on her hips. "Who's going to watch the Govier house if you're over at the Fletchers'?"

"What about you taking a turn, Holly?" I queried. "Who sleeps in the bedrooms at the front of your house, anyway?"

"My parents are in one, and the other is a guest room." She thought about what I was suggesting. "Okay, I guess that's doable," she admitted after a moment or two. "I can give you a break tonight, Martin. I'll sneak into the guest room and watch from there, once Mom and Dad turn in."

Everyone seemed happy with the decision, and it was surprising how much it cheered up the Grange.

At ten o'clock that night, Granger and I were lying on top of our sleeping bags, our heads at the opening of his new tent, watching fireflies blink around the edges of the property. It was an awesome tent, but as a substitute for a camping trip with his dad, it just didn't cut it.

We had devoured the big bag of potato chips Granger had provided, and now we were both thirsty. "I'm going to get us some cans of cola," I said, crawling out of the tent. Mom had left the back door open at home in case I needed anything.

At my place, I retrieved two cans of pop, giving the door of the fridge a hip check to shut it. I had to persuade Lulu to go back to her bed, and then I closed the door of the house again softly. Just on a hunch, I decided to check the Govier place myself. I slid along in the shadows between our house and the next, a can of cola in each hand. As I had expected, the big house across the road was in total darkness. It was Holly's turn to be disappointed. Or maybe she too would be convinced that I'd only imagined the lights.

Suddenly, above me and to my left, a cigarette glowed red in the dark. I pressed myself against the house next door, my heart hammering. I wasn't the only one out there that night! The man in the wheelchair was watching from his front porch.

Scampering barefoot back across the yard, I slipped into the tent, dropping the flap behind me. I shoved a can of pop towards Granger. "I checked the Govier house for lights," I gulped.

"See anything?" Granger ripped the tab off his pop can.

"No, but you know that weird guy who lives next door? He's sitting out on his porch. In the dark!"

"I was the one who told you he was weird, remember?" Granger said.

"You don't suppose he's watching the same house we are, do you?"

Granger shook his head. "Why would he?"

"Maybe he saw the lights too and is wondering about them."

"Nah," said Granger, burping loudly and lying back down on his sleeping bag. "Likely he just couldn't sleep."

"You could be right," I agreed, yawning. It *was* a hot night. I wiped the grass off my wet feet on my sleeping bag and lay down myself.

*   *   *

"You guys!" Suddenly, someone threw aside the flap on our tent. There, framed in the glare of the morning sun, stood Holly, looking fierce. "You were supposed to meet me in the pool at nine o'clock!" Granger and I groaned and covered our faces.

"I'm the one who stayed up half the night, and you two are still sleeping!" she fumed.

"Well, you didn't see the lights, did you?" I demanded, squinting into the sun.

"Oh yes, I did!"

"What?" Granger and I both sat bolt upright.

"Not till nearly midnight, but I saw them. First downstairs, then up."

"All right!" exclaimed Granger, grinning at me.

"No kidding? Okay," I said, "now we take action. Right? Give us a couple of minutes, and we'll be over to the pool."

"Forget that." Holly made a face. "Dad's decided to take all the leaves out of the pool this morning, wash the walls down and see how much repair work has to be done." She sighed. "Just come to the house when you're ready."

"What kind of action, do you think?" Granger asked, struggling into his gym shorts after Holly had left.

"I'm not sure," I admitted. But this was what we'd been waiting for. "We'll have to put our heads together and come up with a plan."

I tied the cord around my rolled up sleeping bag. "Meet you over at Holly's," I said, hoisting the bag onto my shoulder. It felt good to have our mission underway.

Holly was sitting on my back deck when I got home, gabbing away with my parents in the shade of the patio umbrella.

"Good morning, sweetheart," called Mom as I climbed the back stairs. "Make yourself some toast and come out here with us."

I gave myself a quick wash, pulled on a clean T-

55

shirt, and by the time I got back to the deck with two pieces of toast layered with jam, Granger too had joined them.

Dad poured himself another cup of coffee and put his feet up on the railing, opening the weekend paper across his lap. Sunday morning, and the place was crawling with parents! Holly, Granger and I retreated to the front porch.

"So, what are we going to do about this business at the Govier house?" Holly demanded when we'd pulled our chairs in close.

"You were the one who said we were going to take action," I reminded her. "We figured you must have a plan in mind."

"I still think we should tell the police," Granger fretted. His voice rose a little higher. "Maybe it's the ghost of the murdered guy come back to look for something he left behind."

"Or maybe it's the murdered guy, and he's not dead," I countered. "Never was."

Holly was busy with her own thoughts. "Whoever it is seems to be looking for something. The way the light moves from room to room. Don't you agree, Martin?"

"Exactly. And the way I see it, there's only one way to find out what's going on." I felt reckless. "We have to go over there the next time we see the light and confront whoever it is."

"Count me out!" exclaimed Granger, sitting

upright, with a jerk. "That means going over there at night!"

"You're not scared, are you?" Holly asked him. "Because the Deep End Gang has to be together on this."

"Of course not. But I throw up when I get upset. You know that, Holly, better than anyone." Seeing the look on Holly's face, I didn't ask her to explain. "Don't you think we could do it in the daylight?" Granger pleaded.

"Well, maybe a confrontation's not such a good idea," Holly admitted, looking at me as if she were hoping I'd agree. "I mean, you never know who might be in there. Maybe we should do some reconnaissance first."

"I suppose we *could* just wander over there now," I suggested. "Check the doors and stuff while it's light. See if they have been tampered with. That would rule out Granger's theory about a ghost."

"Sounds good." Holly nodded. "But not today."

"Why not? It's still early."

"Sundays are just too busy in this neighbourhood. People mowing lawns, having barbecues. Everyone's outside. We'd be seen."

"Okay," I agreed, "what about tomorrow?"

"No," Holly said. "It's going to have to wait a couple of days. I have to go for an adjustment on my braces tomorrow."

I scowled at her. "Again?"

"I go every month, you know," she said. "And then we're spending two nights at my grandmother's in Thunder Bay."

"That's okay," Granger assured her. "We can wait, can't we, Martin?"

Holly shot him a sharp glance. "But just as soon as I get back, we go over and check the place out. Agreed?"

"We'll be ready," I promised.

Nine

On Tuesday, my sister disappeared. When she didn't come down at her usual time in the morning, Mom went to investigate and found the bed neatly made up and Susan gone.

My sister had vanished, without leaving a clue. Or at least, not one that I knew about before I went to spread the news of her disappearance. This was pretty interesting stuff. Nothing like this had ever happened in our family before.

I decided to forego my usual hearty breakfast, grabbed a juice box from the fridge and went out through the back to Granger's. I only wished Holly could be there to hear me spill all the gory details.

To my disappointment, Granger's mother told me he'd gone to the corner store to buy some milk for their breakfast. "He shouldn't be long, dear," she promised. "Although he had a flat tire on his bike, so he *is* walking."

When I hesitated before turning away from her door, she asked: "Is everything all right, Martin?

You look a little down in the dumps this morning."

I hung my head sorrowfully. "People are disappearing all over the place in this town," I said. Mrs. Fletcher frowned. "Now, it's my own sister."

That got her attention. "Oh my goodness, that's dreadful!" Naturally, Granger's mother wanted to know all about it. "Come inside, dear," she urged, drawing me into her kitchen, pulling a stool out from the island. "Now tell me, is there anything I can do? Have you called the police?"

"Not yet," I admitted. "Susan hasn't been gone twenty-four hours." I remembered hearing somewhere that a person had to be gone for a certain length of time before she officially became a missing person.

"But Susan's only a child!" Mrs. Fletcher exclaimed. "That can't be right!"

Crystal appeared in the kitchen then, shaggy-haired, rubbing her eyes. As I had expected, her reaction to my news was one of shock. Susan had given Crystal no indication that she was planning to run away.

"I'll send Granger over the minute he gets back," his mother promised. "And please tell your mother to call me if I can help in any way." I retreated across the lawn to my house with a niggling fear that I might have said too much.

As it turned out, Susan had left a note for Mom and Dad, saying that she was okay, that she was using her babysitting money and going back to

Winnipeg for a few days. She would be staying at Rebecca's. And please not to worry. She promised to phone as soon as she got there.

Still, Mom was upset. It was pretty mean of Susan to slip out of the house after we'd all gone to bed. She was likely halfway to Winnipeg before Dad left for work this morning. He hurried right back home again after Mom called him. And that's when they discovered the note. It must have blown off the desk when Mom first opened the door to Susan's room that morning. By the time they found it, I'd already let Mrs. Fletcher and Crystal in on the news.

Oh well, I thought, the way I told it was much more exciting. Would it hurt to let the Fletchers share the Jessups' drama for a while? They'd hear about the note soon enough. Then the story would lose all its intrigue. I had forgotten about the snowball effect.

Mom intended to stay by the phone all day, she said, waiting for Susan's call. She kept insisting Susan was too young to be making that long bus trip on her own, especially since she would have been travelling all night, and Dad kept trying to reassure her that she would be fine, that bus drivers kept an eye on young people travelling alone. "No need to be frightened, Jude," he said.

"She's fourteen years old, Raymond! Of course I'm frightened!" Mom's freckles stood out starkly in her pale face.

From the deck where I was waiting, I saw the Grange loping across the back. I waylaid him before he could reach our place. "Mom and Dad are really freaking out in there," I explained, nodding towards the house.

Granger was sympathetic. "Did they call all her friends back in Winnipeg?" he asked. "To see if that's where she went?"

"I'm sure that's the first thing they thought of," I told him. "Look, I'd better get back inside with them."

"Just a minute, Martin." Granger clutched at me suddenly. "You don't suppose, I mean, I just had this horrible thought. What if Susan's been kidnapped?" Talk about *my* overactive imagination!

That's when I realized this was definitely getting out of hand. I should have told him right then that we knew where my sister was. But I didn't. I was too busy enjoying the attention our family drama was getting us.

The next thing I knew, a police cruiser pulled up to the curb in front of our place. The officer mounted the porch, and my dad went to meet him. Gripped by fear, I stood just inside the door and heard the man in uniform say: "I understand there's a problem here, a missing person?" What had I done? Me and my big mouth! "I can file a report for you, save you coming down to the station," the policeman offered.

I crept on silent feet towards the stairs, trying to make my escape before Dad got back inside. Fortunately for me, he had to go first and answer a knock at the back door.

"If there's anything I can do." It was Mrs. Fletcher's voice this time. "I've spoken to someone who offered to print up flyers for you. All we need is a recent photo. And I've been rounding up the neighbours. We'll all join any search party."

I didn't stay around to hear any more. I'd done it again.

*   *   *

"Martin, how could you?" Seconds later, Mom and Dad barged into my bedroom where I lay, pretending to read. "What were you thinking of?"

I kept my eyes on the book. It was easier than looking at them. "I guess I wasn't thinking," I mumbled.

"You got that right!" growled Dad.

"But Mom, Dad, I didn't know Susan had left you a note when I went over to the Fletchers'."

"You were in an awful hurry to spread the news," Dad remarked. I didn't think he wanted to hear Susan's theory for my problem. But the truth is that any news, good or bad, made us a more interesting family.

"Well, now you can just go and tell all those people Mrs. Fletcher contacted that we know where Susan is."

"I can't do that, Mom! I'd feel stupid."

"Well?" said Dad, pointedly.

"You've got to undo the damage you've done," Mom insisted.

"I didn't do any damage!" I swung my legs over the side of the bed and sat up quickly. "I only told two people! It was Mrs. Fletcher who told everyone else."

"Out of concern for us," Mom reminded me. "When you knew about Susan's note, you should have been just as quick in telling Granger's mother the situation was under control as you were in spreading the news in the first place. Letting them go on thinking Susan had 'disappeared' was the same as lying."

I was guilty. I stared down at my bare feet, my toes digging into the carpet.

"You know, Martin," Mom went on, "the way I see it, what you did trivializes the real tragedy of missing children."

"I didn't mean to do that!" I met their eyes, feeling truly ashamed.

"Okay, then. Get moving." Dad gestured me though the bedroom door. "Tell the neighbours that we know where Susan is, and that she's getting the next bus back."

"She is? So soon?"

My parents waited for me to lead the way down the stairs and out the back door. Over at the Fletchers', I met several of our neighbours just as they were leaving. They shook my hand and expressed their relief when I told them that Susan was okay.

From her command post in her kitchen, Mrs. Fletcher listened to my explanation that I hadn't known about the note when I came over with the news. I said I was sorry for alarming her, but I suspected that Granger's mother might have enjoyed rallying the troops to find my sister. Maybe she too needed a little excitement in her life.

It was just as well that the Valentines were away. That was one less neighbour I had to confess to.

I was coming back up Birch Boulevard when I saw the athletic-looking guy come out of the front door of Sam Deitz's house, carrying what looked like a folding table. I was pretty certain Mrs. Fletcher would not have alerted our reclusive next-door neighbour.

"Hi," I called, coming to the edge of the ramp that led off the far side of the porch. "You need a hand with that? Whatever it is?"

"It's a massage table." The man shook his head. "No, thanks. My car's right there. It's no problem."

"I didn't know whether the lady out behind

might have told you about my sister," I said, backing away to let him descend the ramp.

"Your sister?"

"Okay. I guess she didn't."

"Didn't what?"

I nodded in the direction of the Fletchers'. "I mean Mrs. Fletcher, she didn't come over and tell you." He still looked puzzled and a little irritated at being waylaid.

"For a while this morning we thought my sister had disappeared, run away," I explained.

"No kidding?" The man kept walking, and I followed. "And now?" he asked over his shoulder.

"Well, we found a note she'd left, saying she'd taken the bus to Winnipeg."

"So, that's okay then?"

"Well, Mrs. Fletcher sort of went around telling the neighbours, in case they'd seen her, you know. But what Mrs. F. didn't know was that we'd found Susan's note."

By this time we'd arrived at the spot where the red Corvette was parked. Wanting to be helpful, I held the door open while the man slid the massage table into the small space behind the front seat. "I guess you use that table for Mr. Deitz, right?"

"Right."

I nodded. "He doesn't say much, does he?"

"No, he's a very private person." The man got

in under the steering wheel, gripping it with a pair of meaty hands.

"I guess kids kind of get on his nerves, right?"

"Could be," the attendant said, and, pulling the car door shut, he gunned the engine and sped off, leaving me standing in the road, the throaty roar of the twin exhausts in my ears. I watched as he made a left at the next intersection, then heard him shift gears once.

As I turned up our front walk, I was surprised that I could still hear the rumble of the car in the distance, not fading away as I'd expected it would. He had not gone as far as the Townline Road before he'd made the turn. He was still here, somewhere in Birch Gardens.

On a hunch, I took off in the opposite direction, cut across at the corner and arrived at the next street in time to see the red Corvette turn into a driveway about halfway up the block.

By the time I reached the house, the garage door was rolling down behind the car. Why would anyone drive to work if he lived so close, I puzzled? He wasn't lugging that table in and out every day, and at most it was a three-minute walk.

I heard the man kill the engine, and a few seconds later, while I tried to blend in with the birch trees on the boulevard, I saw him leave the garage and enter the house by a side door.

There was a sign on the front of the house,

between the porch light and the brass mailbox: "Chloe Jones-Isbister. Herbologist."

*   *   *

Mom and Dad went to meet Susan's bus the next evening. All three of them were sipping on chocolate shakes when they pulled into the driveway again. They had remembered to buy one for me, but by the time I got it, it had mostly melted.

The way I heard it, Susan's return to Winnipeg had been a painful experience for her. None of her friends had been especially happy about the surprise visit. What hurt the most, she admitted, other than the fact that she had disappointed Mom and Dad, was that Rebecca and Brittany had plans they weren't prepared to cancel just because Susan had shown up. I had to feel sorry for her.

After a few days, my sister became quite philosophical about it, reminding anyone who would still listen that the old saying "you can't go home again" is very true. Maybe we both learned a lesson from that episode. And after that, Susan became almost human.

Ten

L etter for you." Susan tossed a white envelope onto the table in front of me. It slid to a stop against the jar of peanut butter. Who would be sending me a letter, I wondered? Could I have been wrong about my old friends?

I didn't recognize the handwriting—an elegant script in black ink.

Mr. Martin Jessup
2360 Birch Blvd
Branch, Ont.

Two French sevens in the postal code.

Inside, on one folded sheet of paper, was a single sentence: "Stay away from the Govier house."

"What?" This was a gag, right? I checked both sides of the paper. Oh sure, this was Holly's idea of a joke.

Wanting to share Holly's twisted sense of humour with Granger, I strolled over to his house, shaking my head bemusedly.

My friend was mowing the grass. Now that the

poison ivy had cleared up, Granger was expected to do his regular chores, sweat or no sweat. He shut off the machine when he saw the grin on my face, and we sauntered into the shade against the house while Granger read the letter.

"If you shut that thing off, you'll never get it started again," Granger's mother shrilled from the patio door. "Oh, hi, Martin." She waggled her fingers at me and moved back inside.

Granger looked up after reading the note, his eyes huge. "Okay," he gulped. "That does it. I think we should take this seriously."

"Come on, Grange! I'm betting it's from Holly. Here, wait a minute!" I snatched the envelope back from him. "No, I guess it can't be. The postmark is here in Branch. But she could have mailed it on her way out of town." I looked into his pinched, frightened face. "Look, Granger, she's messing with us. Don't let this make you chicken out."

"You don't have to put it like that," he protested. "I'm just trying to be sensible. Going onto that property will be trespassing, you know. There used to be a sign in the driveway."

"Well, it looks as if there's already somebody trespassing over there," I told him. "And no one has bothered to hook the chain with the sign on it across the drive again. Besides, in order for the Deep End Gang to get to the bottom of this, we might have to bend a few rules."

Granger's eyes narrowed. "You mean, you aren't going to heed the warning?"

"Heed the warning? I better not find out you sent this, Granger!" But he looked so dismayed at the suggestion that I knew he hadn't.

*   *   *

When Granger and I saw the Valentines' van turn into their driveway on Wednesday afternoon, we gave Holly just enough time to help carry the bags into the house before we slipped through the hedge to confront her.

"Hey, you guys," she hailed us, jumping down out of the back of the vehicle where she'd been rummaging.

We returned her cheery greeting with twin scowls. "Granger and I have called an emergency meeting of the Deep End Gang," I informed her. "Immediately."

"Okay," Holly said agreeably. "Just let me put this trash in the bin, and I'll be right out."

Two minutes later, Holly plopped down onto one of the chairs in the pool and stuck her sturdy legs out in front of her. "Okay. What's up?" she smiled, revealing the new purple elastics on her braces. I thrust the letter at her.

"When did you get this?" she demanded, reading its terse message.

"Depends," I said. "When did you send it?"

"What? I didn't send it. What makes you think I'd do that?"

"Oh, I don't know," I said, airily. "Just to test Granger and me. See if we're up to your challenge."

"Well, I didn't send it, Martin. But I see what you're getting at. It's natural to suspect one of us sent it. Who else knew what our plans were?"

"Well, if you didn't send it and I didn't send it, that only leaves you, Martin," Granger pointed out.

"Oh, right! I sent myself a warning."

"Stranger things have happened," said Holly. "Maybe you thought it would scare me off, and then you wouldn't have to go over there with me."

"Wait a minute," I protested. "I'm no chicken! Anyway, this is stupid. Let's stop accusing each other and think about this. Did either of you tell anyone what we were going to do?"

They both shook their heads solemnly. "We swore, remember?"

"Right. Okay," I said, speaking slowly as it dawned on me. "And where were we when we were making our plans to go check out the house?"

"Right here, in the pool," said Granger.

I shook my head. "No, we weren't. We were on my front porch. Your dad was working on the pool that day, remember, Holly? And sitting out there on his front porch was..."

"Mr. Deitz!" cried Holly, grabbing her throat

with both hands.

"Exactly! He must have overheard us, and for some reason he doesn't want us to go snooping around the house."

"But why?" from Granger.

"Beats me." I shrugged. "But he's the only one who could have sent that letter, because he's the only one who could have heard us talking."

"It doesn't make sense," Holly insisted. "It's not like he's a policeman or anything. Why would he even care?"

"Well, maybe there's something in that house he doesn't want us to see," I suggested. "Come to think of it, what do you guys really know about him, anyway?"

"Not much," admitted Holly.

"Has he always lived there? Would he know what was in that house?"

"No way," said Granger. "He only moved in a few months before you did."

"About all we know about him is his name," Holly realized.

"I never even knew that, till Holly told you," Granger said. "When he moved in, Mom went over with some muffins, to make him welcome. But he said he wasn't looking for friendly neighbours, that he just wanted to be left alone."

"Then why move here?" queried Holly. "If you don't like other people, you should buy a house way out in the county, in the middle of nowhere."

"My guess is that he picked that place because of the ramps for his wheelchair," I said.

"Uh-uh." Granger shook his head. "Those were built just before he arrived. They did some renovations inside the house too—made doorways wider, tore up the carpeting. Mom only had time for a quick look 'round before she was shown the door."

"I've never seen the man do anything, go anywhere, have you?" I asked.

"Well, he *is* in a wheelchair," said Granger.

"So's my grandfather," I told them. "And the thing he likes best is to be taken for a walk or for a ride in the car. Not plunked in the same spot every day."

"He's some kind of a writer, I think," Holly remembered. "At least, that's what he told my dad when we offered to take him to the block barbecue on the May two-four weekend. Dad thought that explained his need for peace and quiet."

"Have you ever seen him writing anything?" I demanded.

"No. But maybe he's hatching a plot. Don't writers do that?"

"Or maybe," I suggested in an eerie tone, "Mr. Deitz is here for some sinister purpose."

"There isn't too much sinister going on in Branch," Holly snorted.

"No? What about your unsolved murder?"

"Yeah, but that was years ago," said Granger. "Deitz didn't even live here then."

"Okay. It must be something else, then."

Mr. Valentine had left a pile of sticks in the corner of the pool after his cleanup. I drew one towards me and began to peel the bark while I thought about the situation. "There's another strange thing, too," I said. "Deitz has that guy who looks like a WWE wrestler coming in for a while every morning. Then he leaves and comes back again late in the afternoon."

"So?"

"Well, yesterday I followed him when he left. Do you know where he went?"

They both shook their heads.

"Right over to the next block! Almost directly behind the Govier place."

"Maybe he has another client there," Holly suggested. "He's a therapist or something, my mother said."

"He wasn't visiting a client; he walked right into the house. It must be where he lives. He put the 'Vette in the garage there. And why does Deitz have him come in anyway?" I wondered. "He can obviously move that wheelchair around by himself, because he was back out on his porch the other night, after the guy had taken him inside and left."

"What are you suggesting?" asked Holly,

frowning. "That the therapist doesn't know he can get around?"

"I'm not suggesting anything. Just speculating. But it seems to me that Deitz is waiting for something to happen, the way he sits there all the time, looking over at the house."

"What can happen in an empty house?"

"It isn't always empty, though, is it? Someone goes in there with a flashlight." I stood and hurled the stick to the far end of the pool, my mind made up. "I say we go ahead with our plan to check the place out. If whoever is getting in has a key, then we'll have to assume they aren't doing anything illegal. We should at least be able to find out if the doors or windows have been tampered with."

"Right," said Holly, checking her watch. "It's four o'clock now. When do you want to do it?"

"Wait a minute, you guys!" Granger jumped to his feet. "Mr. Deitz is sitting right out there on his porch! I saw him."

"Then, we go when we know Deitz isn't watching. Okay?" Holly fixed us both with a narrow-eyed look.

"Okay," I agreed. "Let's go over to my place and hang out on the porch till the time is right."

"That's a bit obvious," Holly demurred.

"Well, we could have a game of Monopoly or something while we wait. Susan and Crystal left the board out on the table there. The minute Deitz goes inside, we go over to the Govier house."

Our plan in place, the Deep End Gang took up position on our front porch. We bent over the Monopoly board, feverishly exchanging paper money and moving our pieces towards Boardwalk, all the while keeping a close eye on the figure next door. We waited. Within a half-hour, the well-muscled attendant arrived in the Corvette and wheeled Sam inside.

The instant the door closed behind them, we scuttled across the street and hid behind one of the pillars at the entrance to the property.

"All clear," whispered Holly, after we'd given ourselves time to catch our breath. "Stay together now and make a run for those bushes across the driveway."

The three of us left the protection of the pillar and raced down the drive, diving into some overgrown lilacs about halfway to the house. "Okay, now," Holly decided, "you guys go around the far side, checking the doors and windows there. I'll take this side, and we'll meet again at the back of the house."

Granger and I nodded. "Ready to make a run for it?" I asked him.

Suddenly, Granger caught my sleeve. "What if Crystal comes looking for us?" he gasped.

"Why would she?" I demanded. "Susan went

over to see if she wanted to go to the mall."

"Oh, right."

Ahead, the yellow brick house loomed, veiled in shadows, its curtained windows revealing no secrets. Wooden steps led up to a double entrance door. Someone had attached a latch across the opening, fastening it with a padlock.

At Holly's signal, Granger and I scurried like beetles to the far side of the house, flattening ourselves to the wall there. Above us, all the windows on the ground floor had been fixed with iron security bars. We crept cautiously along the side of the house, passing a cement stairwell that led down to the cellar and meeting Holly again at the back.

"Nothing," she reported, wiping cobwebs off her arms. "The screens on the porch are ripped, so I got in and checked the side door. It's latched, like the front. And all the windows have bars on them."

At the back of the house, we were hidden from the next street by an overgrowth of shrubs and large trees. Bushes with shiny black berries almost concealed the rear entrance to the house, but I managed to push my way through to reach an outer screen door. It opened easily. The knob on the solid wooden door inside, however, refused to turn in either direction.

"It's locked," I called to the others.

Holly too had made her way through the bushes

and was now peering in through one of the back windows, her hands cupped to the sides of her face. "No curtains or blinds here," she reported. "Have a look."

Granger and I positioned ourselves at the barred window on the other side of the door. Inside, we could see a plain, old-fashioned kitchen with wooden cupboards and a counter, a green fridge and a cook stove with a pipe going into a brick chimney. There was a table with four chairs in the middle of the room and a closed door in the wall that faced us. Next to it was the entrance to a dark hallway.

One of the kitchen chairs had been pulled out from its place, and there were two crushed aluminum cans on the table.

"Very interesting," I said, giving the word all four of its syllables.

"Someone was in there, that's for sure," declared Holly from her window. "But how did they get in?"

"They would have to have had a key to get in through the front or side or back doors," I said. "But there is another door that we didn't try."

"Which one?" Holly asked, surprised.

"The one into the cellar. Come on and we'll show you."

We crept back to the east side of the house, keeping tight to the wall and dropping down into the stairwell Granger and I had earlier observed. The steps down to the door into the cellar were crumbling, and spindly weeds struggled up through the broken cement.

"Wait a minute!" Granger balked. "This goes into the basement! Even if it isn't locked, it'll be awfully dark inside. We didn't bring any flashlights."

I was crouched in the stairwell, one step above him. "Okay, move aside, then," I said. "I'll try it."

I dropped to the bottom of the steps and reached for the doorknob. It turned easily under my grasp, and the door swung inward.

Eleven

Holly and I had left Granger scrunched on the top step of the stairwell, his long, skinny legs folded awkwardly under him. Down in the cellar, draped in cobwebs, pipes from an ancient heating system snaked across the low ceiling. There were some windows at ground level, but these were small and let in a minimum of light.

I stepped cautiously into the room, wishing I'd brought a flashlight. It took me a few seconds to realize that, except for a path through to the stairs, the area was completely filled with piles of bundled newspapers and stacks of boxes in every imaginable shape and size.

Directly opposite the cellar entrance, a set of narrow stairs led up to a closed door on the first floor. Behind the open stairs were shelves of dusty preserving jars, some still filled with murky contents.

"Did you notice?" Holly's voice came from behind me. "There are no cobwebs around this entrance? This has to be how they are getting in."

Not to mention the fact that the door wasn't locked.

Before I had a chance to remind her of that, and to tell her that by standing in the doorway she was blocking the light, we heard someone calling out on the street. "Granger! Where are you, Granger?"

The third member of the Deep End Gang dropped down to the bottom of the stairwell. "You guys!" he croaked, "my mother's looking for me!"

"Rats!" exclaimed Holly. "Wouldn't you know it?" She gave a desperate look around. "What do you think, Martin?"

"I guess we've got to go," I said. "We can't risk her finding us here. Or alerting the whole neighbourhood."

We had no choice. I followed the others back into the stairwell and daylight, pulling the cellar door shut behind me. Then the Deep End Gang darted up the steps and ran out through the Goviers' back yard to the next block. From here we could circle back to our street.

"Hey, hang on a sec," I hailed the others as we cut through the yard behind Govier's. "I know this place!" They turned anxious faces towards me. "This is where Deitz's attendant lives!"

There was a window in the top of the side door into the garage. "Can you see anything? I asked Holly, who was closest to it.

"I can if I jump," she determined. "Nope. It's

empty." And she hurried out to the sidewalk, where Granger was doing an impatient little dance.

"Let me see," I insisted, springing up to take a look myself. There was no car inside. Something wasn't right. I glanced at my watch. It was ten after five.

"Will you hurry up, Martin?" Holly urged.

"I think the guy who looks after Deitz lives here," I explained as we scurried on down the block. "Chloe what's-her-name must be his wife."

"Dr. Jones-Isbister isn't married," said Granger.

"She's a doctor?"

"Kind of. She's treating Mom for her migraines. And she definitely lives here on her own."

Two minutes later, we had circled back to our block, slowing our pace as we drew closer. Strolling up Birch Boulevard, we could see Sam Deitz back out on the porch in his usual position. Why the change of plans today, I wondered? The red Corvette was idling at a low rumble by the curb, and the attendant was sitting on the railing of the porch, watching us approach.

Granger's mother and Mrs. Valentine were standing in Holly's front yard. "Where were you, anyway?" Mrs. Fletcher demanded. She didn't wait for an answer. "Your sister called from the mall, and they've got those sneakers you wanted on sale, Granger. Today only. You needed them for back to school." Obviously, our investigations were over for the day.

Holly and I corralled Granger before he could follow his mother through the opening in the hedge. "Meet us at the pool tomorrow afternoon. Okay?" Holly muttered. "As soon as Mr. Deitz goes inside, we're going back over."

"We'll get up into the house next time, Grange," I added. "So bring a flashlight!" Out front, Deitz's attendant punched the accelerator of the Corvette, and we heard it roar off down the street.

Holly and I wandered listlessly out back to the pool, our adrenaline drained. Mr. Valentine was patching the concrete and had set our chairs up onto the grass, propping the three-legged table against a tree. "We're going to have to find another place to meet, by the looks of it," I lamented, looking down at the spotty walls of the pool before I collapsed in the shade.

"That won't happen any time soon," Holly promised. She took her comb out of her hair, checked it for cobwebs and, scraping her damp bangs off her forehead, put it back in again. "Dad says we can put the chairs back down as soon as the patches are dry."

She became thoughtful. "I never figured it would be so easy to get inside the Govier house, Martin. Did you? Almost too easy, don't you think?"

"What do you mean?"

"Well, why would the house be open? All those

bars on the windows, and you leave a door unlocked?"

"Could have been by accident," I said.

"Or it could have been on purpose."

"You mean, like someone wants somebody to get in?"

She nodded, looking grim. "Maybe someone's setting a trap, or something."

I hadn't thought of that. I'd just been thankful we hadn't had to break any windows to get in. "Well, I'm sure the trap isn't meant for us," I decided. But it bothered me that Deitz and his attendant were both out on the porch waiting when we got back that afternoon.

Dad had two tickets to a basketball game at the rec centre on the base that night. A team of celebrity players was visiting, and Dad invited me to go with him. After the game, I had trouble falling asleep. I don't think it was just the excitement of the game or the double chocolate sundae from the Diary Dipt. Several times I got out of bed to go to the window and look over at the Govier place. Holly's suggestion that the unlocked door might be a trap had left me with an uneasy feeling that I couldn't shake. Were we walking into danger?

*   *   *

Granger seemed to be taking his time coming over the next day. I suspected he was hoping we would go without him. At four-thirty, I had to go call for him. "Come on!" I urged when I found him lying on his bed, staring at the ceiling. "We don't have much time."

"My mom had all these jobs she wanted me to do," he whined. "Took me all day."

"Yeah, right," I said with sarcasm. "Look, Grange, we've got to get in and out of there fast."

He rolled up onto his feet. "Okay, okay, but I'm bringing this." And he hauled a humungous flashlight out from under the bed.

He got no argument from me. "That's excellent," I agreed.

Holly was pacing the length of the pool when we arrived. "What took you so long?" she fumed. "Your neighbour's already gone inside."

One last look through the cedars at Deitz's house, and the three of us pelted across the street, paused briefly behind the pillar and then raced for the lilacs again. There was still no activity on Sam Deitz's front porch, so we counted to three and scurried across the yard to the stairwell on the far side of the house, dropping down to the cellar door. It was still unlocked. We were in!

"Shut off that flashlight as soon as we get upstairs," Holly ordered. "There'll be enough light up there, and we don't want to attract any attention."

I could feel Granger's clammy hand against my back as we crossed the cellar and ascended the steps to the first floor. The door at the top of the stairs opened into the kitchen we'd seen through the back windows. We moved stealthily into the room. "Might as well start here," Holly decided.

"What are we looking for, exactly?" Granger asked.

"Whatever the intruder was looking for," I said, giving Holly a quizzical look. "Right?"

"Clues," she said. I knew then that she hadn't thought about it either.

"I hope I know a clue when I see one," muttered Granger.

It didn't take long to determine that there was nothing in the dreary kitchen anyone would want to steal. As far as I could tell, the bars on the windows had been added only to give an old lady living alone a sense of security.

We opened cupboards stacked with chipped dishes and glassware and drawers still filled with folded linen and specked with mouse droppings.

The fridge had been emptied and shut off, but it smelled really gross inside. "Yuck!" exclaimed Holly, shutting it quickly.

A calendar showing a basket of orange kittens and the month of October, 1998, was tacked to the wall over the sink. On the opposite wall I spotted a black picture frame and under the glass a newspaper clipping, yellow with age. I stepped closer to read the caption.

UNIVERSITY FRIENDS START BUSINESS IN BRANCH. *Victor Govier, son of Mr. and Mrs. Gordon Govier, and his business partner, Samuel Deitz of Montreal.*

"Holy cow! There's the connection!" I exclaimed. The others crowded in to have a look. "They were business partners! Deitz and the murdered guy!"

Smiling into the camera was a tall, pleasant-faced, blonde-haired youth with wide shoulders and beside him, legs planted in a firm stance, stood a scowling Sam Deitz. They were both dressed in football uniforms, helmets tucked under their arms.

"That's definitely a clue!" exclaimed Granger happily.

But Holly was no longer studying the clipping. "Weren't there two pop cans on the table yesterday when we looked in the window?" she asked uneasily.

"Yes," I said, turning to look myself.

"Well, where are they now?" she croaked. "Someone's been in here since..."

At that very instant we heard the sound of footsteps coming up the cellar stairs.

We stared at each other in wide-eyed terror for a fraction of a second, then swung around and fled down the hall. Each one of the doors we passed in our flight to the front of the house was closed. We tumbled into the living room together, and I saw Holly drop quickly behind a wing chair. Searching frantically for a place to hide myself, I yanked Granger into the space between a loveseat and the opposite corner.

Someone closed the cellar door to the kitchen. We waited, breathless.

"I know you kids are in here," a male voice boomed. "You might as well come out."

"My flashlight!" A sob escaped Granger's throat. "I left it on the counter!"

There was silence for a few moments. Very cautiously, I allowed myself a look around the end of the loveseat. There, muscular arms folded across his chest, stood Sam Deitz's attendant. We were trapped!

Holly was the first to reveal herself. "I thought so," the man said grimly as she came out of hiding.

Granger clung to me so close that I could smell his fear. Slowly, I too stood up, dragging him with me.

The man was standing in the doorway, silhouetted in the light from the kitchen window down the hall, and he looked more powerful than ever. My heart pounded in my ears. We were done for!

"Figured it was you three," growled the man. "Breaking and entering. I ought to call the cops."

"We didn't have to break anything," I said, surprised at finding I could speak at all. "The cellar door was open."

"How did you know we were over here?" Holly asked, her voice reedy.

"Saw you from across the street." He jerked his head in that direction. "Now march! Mr. Deitz is waiting for you."

We were herded out of the house the same way we had come in—down through the cellar and up the outer stairwell into the daylight.

"I have to get home," Granger managed to choke. He was stumbling miserably along between Holly and me. "It's time for supper. I'm not allowed to be late."

Ignoring him, our little procession halted below Deitz's front porch. "Into the house," barked the attendant.

As we mounted the steps, I looked over at my own house, praying someone would see us. Where was everybody when you needed them? My mind was whirling with unanswered questions. Did Victor Govier die at the hands of Sam Deitz? Were we entering the house of a killer? I had the sickening feeling we were about to find out.

The man with the over-developed muscles pushed us through the door and shut it firmly behind him, blocking it with his bulk. Who could come to our rescue now?

Twelve

Sam Deitz was sitting in the east window in his wheelchair, his back to us as we entered the house. The Deep End Gang, our shoulders touching, stood trembling together on the hardwood floor inside the front door.

"Here they are, sir," announced the attendant, a note of triumph in his voice. "Just as we suspected." He set Granger's flashlight on the windowsill in front of Deitz, as if it were evidence.

Slowly, the man in the wheelchair swivelled around to face us, sizing us up with his piercing eyes. It seemed like forever before he spoke. "So," he said, finally, "you chose to ignore my warning."

I had expected his voice to be high-pitched and nasal, like that of Peter Lorre, the sinister little actor in the old movies my dad enjoyed. Instead, it was low and rumbled like thunder, as if it came from some cavern deep inside his body.

"Then you did send me that note?" I asked, swallowing hard.

Deitz nodded. "It seemed the simplest way to handle it. Obviously, I was wrong."

I shifted from one foot to the other, uneasily. Holly cleared her throat. "The cellar door at the house was open, sir," she ventured. "We were only looking around. We didn't hurt anything."

Suddenly, without any warning, Deitz slammed his fist down hard on the arm of his wheelchair, and Holly leapt backwards as if she'd been struck. "I've spent months putting this plan into action!" the man roared. "The last thing I need is a bunch of nosy kids poking around!"

A stunned silence followed the outburst. "We were just curious," I said hoarsely. "We saw lights in the house at night, sir. But the place is supposed to be empty."

"Curiosity kills," the attendant growled. He kept his position between us and the door. "Ever hear of the man who shut himself inside the fridge because he was curious to see if the light went out?"

From Granger's throat came a sound like strangling.

"Thank you, Cyril," nodded Sam Deitz, calm again. (Cyril? I thought.) "You may go back over now. I will endeavour to explain to these young people the consequences of sticking their noses where they don't belong."

"Whatever you say," agreed Cyril, gravely. "If you

need any muscle, sir, you know where to find me."

Deitz tapped the wireless phone in his lap with one swollen finger. "Absolutely," he said.

After the door had shut behind Cyril, Deitz motioned us toward the leather couch under the opposite window. "Sit," he commanded.

The three of us moved to the couch as if we were all one body and perched on its edge. Out on the street, the red Corvette sped away from the curb. I felt myself relax a little after the attendant's departure. After all, three kids could overpower a fat guy in a wheelchair. In any case, it seemed more likely now that the murder had been the work of the well-muscled man named Cyril.

Deitz's expression was grim, but he seemed to have regained control of his temper. "I can't have you getting in the way," he stated simply. When he said nothing more for a while, I realized, with horror, that he was trying to figure out what to do with us.

"I live right next door," I volunteered. Don't ask me why; maybe to cover the sound of Granger swallowing. "I see you sitting on the porch all the time, sir." Deitz fixed me with a dark look.

"What is it that you think we'll get in the way of?" Holly asked, gently.

Deitz shifted the deliberate gaze to her face. "Of someone who is coming back from the dead," he said.

Holly let out an unsteady breath. "Who, sir?" she gasped. "Is it your old friend?"

"Victor Govier?" I offered, determined to be as brave as Holly.

"Indeed," Mr. Deitz nodded. "You kids seem to have it all figured out." He laced his fingers together, stretching his hands outward. We heard the knuckles crack. "Well, I suppose I shouldn't be surprised. What is surprising is that people still remember. Victor's disappearance is old news."

"But it was never solved, sir," I pointed out.

He ignored my interruption and continued to speak as if he were thinking out loud. "It is unfortunate that you've barged in before the mission was complete. You've put the whole thing in jeopardy now.

"I can't risk you telling your parents who, being good citizens, will undoubtedly call the authorities. But what to do with you? That is the question. I can't keep you here, of course. Now, Cyril wanted to call the police and have you charged with trespassing. But what if you had some legitimate suspicions and said as much to the authorities? My plan would never reach its proper conclusion.

"And so," he went on, "I have decided it is probably best to tell you the truth behind what is happening."

The Deep End Gang held its breath.

Sam Deitz gave a shuddering sigh and focussed again on his audience. "Yes, it is Victor I am waiting for."

"Everyone thinks he's dead," said Granger, finding his voice at last.

"Because that's the way Victor wanted it. He made his disappearance look like a robbery and a kidnapping. Possibly a murder." The bald head nodded. "It was a robbery, all right. But he was the thief. He'd been helping himself to the funds from our business for years. Something I didn't find out till after he'd gone."

"Did you know all along where he went?" Holly asked.

"Oh, no. But I always suspected he had planned the whole thing. There was no body, and the police had no evidence to link me to his disappearance. But I was not satisfied. I looked everywhere for him, tracked one lead after another. I wasn't in this wheelchair then," he explained.

"One day, about four years ago and purely by accident, I spotted him. In a theatre, in a small town in Florida where I was vacationing. I found myself sitting several rows behind him. I knew it was him! He had the most annoying habit that I remembered from our days at university. He ate sunflower seeds all the time, but not the way most people eat them. Victor would fill his hand, then give a little flick of his wrist to work one seed down between his thumb and forefinger, before putting it in his mouth. Used to drive me crazy! He couldn't eat sunflower seeds any other way. And it was that flicking that first caught my attention in the theatre. I couldn't believe anyone else ate the same way!

"But I had to be sure. I moved a few rows closer. Even before I saw his face, I knew. I recognized the shape of his head, the set of his shoulders. But I had to be very careful; I didn't want him to run. As he left the theatre, I sneaked a look at his face. It was Victor!

"I followed him outside. Then another lucky break: he was on foot. I trailed him for several blocks until he turned in at a duplex and went inside. After he'd gone in, I checked the names on the two mailboxes at the door. One was for a Carmelita someone-or-other. And the other was for Vincent Gower. He hadn't even had to change his monogrammed cuff links!" His tone was bitter.

"Did you go to the police?" Holly inquired.

Deitz shook his head. "No, I had him where I wanted him, for the time being. I didn't want to spook him. I wanted him to keep thinking that he was safe while I decided what to do next. I'd reel him in on my own when I was ready. Then I'd call the police."

He let out another heavy sigh and continued. "In the meantime, I had a serious car accident and found myself confined to this chair, paralyzed from waist to toe. After that, I had lots of time to think about the trap I was going to set, only now it meant I was going to have to find a way to lure him to me. It became my obsession."

We listened intently as the bizarre tale spun on. "When Victor's mother died three years ago, I thought he might happen to show up, disguised, of course. I came down here to the funeral and studied the crowd. He never came. But how could anyone let him know? Everyone thought he was dead himself.

"So, last spring, I bought this house across from the Govier place and began to put my plan in motion. Now I'm waiting for him to take the bait."

"What makes you think he'll come?" I asked.

"Oh, he'll come. Sometime between now and the sale of the property on September 2nd, he'll come. His greed will bring him. It's a sickness with him, you see. He thinks there's something in that house that's worth some money. So he'll come to get it before the house is sold. All I had to do to lure him back was make him believe his mother had left something of great value behind, something he hadn't known about before."

"And is there?" I inquired. "Something of great value in the house?"

"He thinks there is. I have planted the seed in his greedy mind. The trick was to get the seed to him."

"Cool," I said. "But how did you do that, without him knowing you were behind it?"

"I got hold of the newspaper in the town in Florida where he lived. It took a bit of work. But remember, I've had years to perfect my plan. I wrote a fairly general story about the practice of selling properties for back taxes, how it's sometimes the way a buyer can acquire a house or a piece of property fairly cheaply.

"I did some investigating and got the goods on a couple of homes in that part of Florida that were to be sold for the taxes that were owing on them. And, as an interesting side note, I included the Govier house up here in Canada. I worked in a bit of the sad story behind that particular sale— the kidnapped, only heir, the heartbroken mother. It was fairly simple to get the official list of items that are to be auctioned September 2nd. I doctored the list a little to include an album of rare stamps that doesn't really exist.

"Small town papers are often eager to buy human interest stories. My story used the angle that no one knows what hidden treasures might surface after these sales. I sent for pictures of all the houses, to ensure that Victor knew it was his mother's house that was referred to, however briefly, in the story.

"I sent the story to the paper, using the name of Cyril Jones. I wasn't too surprised when it was turned down. Not of sufficient interest to local readers was the excuse. But I sent it in again, along with a money order for a full-page ad to run all month long for some herbal medicines from a company where Cyril has connections. That changed the editor's mind in a hurry.

"The story ran in the paper in Govier's Florida town a couple of weeks ago. So, the trap is set. And any time now he'll show up to collect what he thinks is his. And when he does, I'll be waiting. Or rather, Cyril will."

"So Cyril's the one who's been over there at night," I realized. "Anyone could have seen his flashlight, you know. I did."

"He doesn't need it now," Deitz said. "At first, before the trap was set, Cyril had to familiarize himself with the inside of the house. I know the layout quite well myself; I used to come here for weekends with Victor years ago. No, now that everything is ready, we have to be more careful. We can't risk Victor suspecting anything."

"But why leave the cellar door open?" I wondered.

"Because we want to be sure that is the door Victor uses," Sam Deitz explained. "We don't want him trying to break in through the back of the house, where we can't see him.

"I watch from my porch during the day, while Cyril gets some sleep at his apartment in town. At night, after he gets me settled, Cyril hides his car and waits inside the Govier house. Timing is everything. This has become a fulltime occupation for me. And Mr. Jones will help me see it through to completion.

"Victor's mother gave me a spare key one time. If ever I was in town, she said, there was always a bed in the house for me. After his disappearance, she must have forgotten that I still had it. I'm not sure she ever knew it was a key to the door into the cellar."

He returned his brooding gaze to our pale faces. "If you kids had stayed away as I'd hoped when I sent you that warning, my plan could have gone off without a hitch. Now, I'm not so sure. When Cyril spotted you going over there, I decided I'd better let you in on it, so that you'd understand the consequences of your interference."

The three of us exchanged worried glances.

"I expect Victor will have a good look around first, to see if there's anyone guarding the place, a security company or something. When he sees that there isn't, he'll go in and start looking for the stamps. And Cyril will be there. I'm only going to confront my former partner after he's caught himself. I want him forced out in the open for the cheat and fraud that he is."

"What if he has a gun?" Holly asked. "If he went to so much trouble to disappear, he might do anything to protect his secret."

"That's why the element of surprise is so important. I don't want to put Cyril's life in danger."

"Of course not," agreed Holly.

"So now the question is, what are we going to do about the three of you?"

"Do, sir?" I queried. "You don't have to *do* anything. You can trust us completely."

"I hope so. Have I made you all sufficiently aware of the seriousness of this venture? How much is depending on its success? If Govier gets away this time, you can be sure he'll never, ever be revealed."

"Absolutely," said Holly, and Granger and I nodded in agreement.

"He must be brought to justice!" declared the Grange.

"And you must swear not to give anyone even a hint of what you know. This thing is almost over. You are to tell no one! Not your families, no other friends."

"We swear," I said. "Right, guys? We have this club, sir, the Deep End Gang. We swear on the honour of our club."

Sam Deitz nodded gravely. "Then I have to trust you. I have no grudge against you youngsters." He laid his pudgy hands on the arms of his chair. "So," he concluded, finally, "you may go now."

Just like that! The three of us stood. My knees felt like jelly.

"Remember the importance of your promise!"

Mr. Deitz pleaded. "And never go near the Govier house again." He held the flashlight towards us. Granger took it, looking stricken.

In silence, we stumped down the front steps, across our yard, and out back to the pool. Granger was the first to speak after we'd dropped onto the chairs. "Holy cow," he shuddered. His eyes were blue saucers. "Do you believe that?"

For once, Holly seemed at a loss for words. "Mr. Deitz is this close to catching him," I marvelled, holding up a thumb and forefinger, an inch apart. "I'd give anything to be there when Govier walks into the trap."

"Me, too," said Holly. "But we can't. We have to respect Mr. Deitz and back off. You know, I feel sorry for him now. He's such a sad man."

"I just hope it won't take too long," Granger admitted. "I don't know whether I can bear the weight of Mr. Deitz's secret for very long."

Holly and I both pounced. "You have to!"

"I know! Geez, don't be so jumpy! I swore, didn't I? What about you, Martin? You're the blabbermouth in the neighbourhood."

I leapt to my feet, knocking over the plastic chair. "You take that back!" I demanded.

"Okay, okay. But you know how you like to talk."

"And I can also keep a secret when I swear to!" I was indignant.

"Listen," said Holly, the voice of reason, "we're all on edge after what just happened, but we need to be very careful. There are three of us in this club, right? None of us has to bear this secret alone. We can talk about it all we want whenever we're here in the deep end. But that's it! Okay? Don't mention it anywhere else. Even if we think no one else is around. That's how we'll handle it. Agreed? This is the only place we blow off steam."

"Agreed," Granger and I chorused. This was definitely serious business now.

"Sorry, Martin," Granger mumbled, studying his size ten feet. He seemed to have forgotten that he was late for supper. When he looked up again, he wore a sheepish smile. "You guys never said how you liked my new sneakers."

"They look good," I allowed, "but I thought they were for back-to-school."

"Well, that's not too far off, you know," replied Granger. He *had* to remind us.

Thirteen

There was an accident on the bridge in town as I was coming home," Dad announced the next evening, searching the dishwasher for a clean plate for his supper. "The rain was really coming down hard at the time."

"We were wondering where you'd gotten to," Mom said. "Was it a bad accident?" She dropped a pork chop onto the proffered plate.

"Pretty bad. The traffic had to back off the bridge to let the ambulance get to the scene. One of the cars involved looked like the one the guy next door drives. The '86 Corvette?"

My ears perked up. "You mean the man who helps Mr. Deitz?"

"I think so," Dad said, settling himself at the table. "It looked like the same car, anyway. They took both drivers to the hospital. More than just a fender-bender."

"Oh, that poor man!" cried Mom. "Mr. Deitz, I mean. How will he manage over there by himself?"

I was wondering the same thing. But I was thinking more along the lines of, who was going to keep watch at the Govier place if Cyril was in hospital?

"You know, Ray," Mom decided, laying down her fork, "I think we should go next door and make sure he's all right."

"I'll go with you," I said. "Granger's mother said he's not very friendly."

Sam Deitz was occupying his usual position on the front porch. "Is everything okay?" Mom called, from the railing at the end of our porch.

Mr. Deitz turned his head and scowled at us.

"There was a car accident in town," Dad explained from over Mom's shoulder. "One of the cars looked like the one your aide drives. Have you heard from him this evening?" By this time, our little band had left our porch and trooped in the rain across the strip of lawn to Deitz's front steps.

"We both have cell phones," said Sam Deitz, frowning. "I'm sure Mr. Jones would contact me if there was a problem."

Dad shook his head, and we ascended the steps. "They took the occupants of both vehicles away in the ambulance."

"I've noticed that your aide is usually here by four-thirty," Mom said. "It's almost six, and I wondered if you'd like to go inside; if I could bring you a plate of supper?"

Deitz was studying my face. I hoped it was obvious from my deliberately blank expression that I hadn't divulged his secret.

"Look," said Mom, gently, "why don't I call the hospital for you, just to make sure? I'm a nurse there part-time. They would tell me if your man was there, and what his condition is. If he isn't coming, I'm sure the agency would send out a replacement."

"That won't be necessary, madam," Deitz said, his tone coldly formal. "Mr. Jones is my physical therapist. I am not totally dependent on him, nor on anyone else. I still have mobility in my upper body and can get myself inside and use a telephone." He made a little bow with his head. "But I thank you," he acknowledged. Subject closed.

When we got back to our house, Mom called the hospital anyway. One of the drivers involved in the accident, they told her, was Cyril Jones. He was still in the emergency room and was being prepared for admission. "Non-life threatening injuries," Mom announced, hanging up the phone.

"I'll just pop out there and make sure Mr. Deitz knows," said Dad.

If Cyril wasn't coming, I realized, someone had to watch the Govier house that night. Since I was the one with the rooftop venue, it might as well be me. The steady rain prevented me from sitting outside on the porch roof, but I pulled a chair up to my window and propped my feet on the sill.

At ten o'clock, I heard Mom and Dad come up to bed. "Mr. Deitz is still out there, Ray," Mom was worrying. "It doesn't seem right."

"Well, we've done all we can," Dad reminded her. "He'll go inside when he's ready."

Only I knew that Sam Deitz had no intention of leaving his post that night. We'd both be watching from our side of the street, but it made me uneasy knowing that there was no one inside the house to catch Victor Govier in the act.

I don't know how late I managed to keep the vigil myself before I started to nod off. I'd jerk awake, feeling guilty, but soon my head would start to fall towards my chest again. Sleep eventually overcame me and, trusting Mr. Deitz to stay awake, I crawled over to my bed where I passed out.

As soon as I opened my eyes the next morning, I leapt to my feet. To my relief, Mr. Deitz was still out on his porch. Had he kept watch all night, I wondered? He was a better watchman than I was, if he had.

The rain had stopped, and the new day was clear and bright. I took my glass of orange juice out front with me. "Morning," I greeted Sam Deitz, before sitting down on our steps. I could see that the man had gone inside at some time last night, long enough to fetch the blanket he now wore around his shoulders.

"You going to be out here long?" he growled, without really looking at me.

"I can be," I offered.

"Very good. I will be right back." He swung the chair around and went inside. Without him asking, I knew he was counting on me to watch the Govier house in his absence.

Within ten minutes, I heard the door of his house open, and he reappeared. "Thank you," he said, wheeling into position.

"No problem," I replied. He seemed to have nothing more to say, and I was anxious to get over to Holly's anyway, to let the other members of the Deep End Gang in on this latest development.

The two of them were sitting on the cement steps in the shallow end of the pool, Granger not wanting to get his new sneakers damp.

"Poor Mr. D.," Holly commiserated, when I told them the news. "This could mess up everything for him. It would be awful if Victor Govier gets away again."

I agreed. "After Mr. Deitz has gone to all this trouble," I said. I looked from one to the other. "You know, you guys, we've got to help him. Who else is there but us?"

"But how?" Holly wondered. "What can we do? He asked us to stay out of it."

"Well, it's easy enough for us to watch from this side of the street, but there's no one in the house to stop Govier. Mom says Deitz's man will likely be released tomorrow. But for tonight, I say we've got to be there in Cyril's place."

"You mean, like, inside the house?" Granger gulped.

"That might be pretty dangerous," Holly cautioned. "What if this is the night Victor Govier chooses to show up? We can't overpower him."

"No, but we can call the police. That's all Mr. Deitz can do," I pointed out. "Maybe we can even lock Govier inside, till the police get there."

They still looked doubtful. "Look," I explained, "if nothing happens, Mr. D. doesn't even need to know we were in there. But at least we'll know all the bases are covered."

"I've got an idea!" Granger offered, brightening. "Why don't we take Lulu with us? She's big enough to scare a burglar."

"We don't want to scare anybody," I said. "We'd never be able to keep Lulu quiet. It'll have to be just us."

"Well, Govier's not likely to come in broad daylight," Holly reasoned. "So I think we're safe till about nine o'clock, don't you? When it gets dark?"

"Right," I agreed. "So, can you guys get out tonight?"

"I can," said Granger. "I'll just say I'm camping out. The tent's still up in the backyard."

"Okay," I nodded. "I'll go camping with you."

"My parents are sound sleepers," Holly told us. "I'll have no problem."

"Okay, then. We'll all meet here at the pool at 8:45 sharp and go over."

"It's up to us now," Holly reminded us, sternly. "Swear to silence!" The Deep End Gang solemnly slapped palms to seal it.

Granger went home then, deciding he needed to rest up for the night's adventure. Intending to do likewise, Holly and I strolled back towards her house and the opening in the hedge.

"Before you came over, Martin," Holly said, keeping her tone casual, "Granger was telling me that Susan ran away, while I was at my grandmother's."

"She didn't really run away," I objected.

"She went back to Winnipeg without your parents' permission, didn't she?"

"Right."

"So, that's running away."

"Okay, whatever," I shrugged. "Anyway, it didn't work out the way she had hoped."

"What happened?"

"I guess it took her about five minutes to find out her old friends were doing okay without her. Susan thought they'd be so happy to see her. Instead, they made her feel like an outsider."

We'd reached the Valentines' back door, but

Holly hesitated before going inside. "Does she hate it here that much?" she wondered.

"I guess she did," I said. "It wasn't that there was anything wrong with Branch. She would have hated any place that wasn't Winnipeg. But she's okay with it now."

I turned to leave, but Holly persisted. "Do you think you'll be like that, Martin, about moving from here, when you're Susan's age?"

"Likely not."

"Why?"

"Guys are just different."

"I think it's more an age thing than a gender thing," Holly stated.

"You're the expert," I told her and made another move towards home.

"So, you won't even miss the Grange and me when you move?"

"I didn't say that." I frowned. "It's just that I'm usually too busy hanging out with my new friends to spend much time thinking about the old ones."

"Humph!" Holly snorted. "That's kind of heartless!"

"I don't know why you're getting all bent out of shape about this," I admitted, my voice rising. "I'm the one who does the moving, not you."

"Well, I've just been thinking," Holly went on, playing with the door latch. "You said that moving all the time didn't really bother you. But

I figure, you have to be affected by it." (Holly the shrink, I thought.) "Look at the way you said you try to impress people, so that they'll like you, want to be your friend."

I wished she wouldn't keep bringing that up. "You know the best kind of friends for a guy like me to have?" I demanded, not really wanting to hurt her, but wanting to stop the analysis. "The kids that live on the base. They hang out together while they can, knowing that after a while some of them will be posted. They might meet again on another base, or they might not. And it doesn't really matter."

Holly had ducked inside by this time. "I just wanted to tell you that Granger and I will miss you, Martin," she said, before closing the door.

I made my way over to my place, feeling awful. Was Holly right? Was I heartless? I'd always figured that if my old friends missed me at all, it wouldn't be for long. I pictured them saying, within days of my leaving: "Remember that kid who used to live here? What was his name? Martin somebody-or-other?" And what Susan discovered when she went back to Winnipeg only served to prove my point.

* * *

"He's asleep, poor thing," said Mom, returning to

our house from next door after supper. "I left the plate of sandwiches beside him but didn't have the heart to waken him."

By the time the Deep End Gang made its dash across the street, Mr. Deitz was snoring loud enough to be heard over on our front porch. All the hours without sleep had caught up with him.

At 8:55 we were standing inside the cellar door of the Govier house, hearts pounding, afraid even the sounds of our breathing might alert someone to our whereabouts. But there was silence all around us. The house, I was sure, was empty.

Since I was in the lead, Granger had given me his flashlight. I fumbled with it until I found the button and clicked it on. Something small rustled away into the corner.

"What was that?" gasped Granger. Holly answered him with a sharp poke to the ribs, her lips pursed severely.

We shuffled our way across the floor to the foot of the stairs. A sliver of moonlight showed under the kitchen door above us. Very cautiously, lifting one foot to the step above and testing it before putting my full weight on it, I ascended the stairs, the others close behind.

At the top, I turned the knob and eased the door open, shutting off the flashlight. Moonlight flooded the kitchen. The other two slipped into the room behind me. I closed the cellar door, not releasing the knob until the door was in place, to avoid making a sound. We slid along the line of cabinets and down the hall.

At the front of the house, the living room, with its closed curtains, was almost dark. We knew the location of the furniture from our previous daytime visit. Standing in a tight group, we waited till our eyes became accustomed to the dim light. This, we had already determined, was where we would take up our vigil.

"Now what?" Granger whispered.

"Find a place to sit," I suggested.

"Just don't make yourself too comfortable," Holly warned. "We have to stay awake till morning."

Tiptoeing across the room, I lifted aside the curtain on the front window only enough to see outside. The sight of the familiar houses across the street was comforting, until I remembered that everyone over there would soon be on his way to bed, or like Sam Deitz, was already fast asleep.

"Can you see him from here?" whispered Granger, who must have been thinking the same thing I was. He came up behind me, and I held the drapery open a bit wider for him.

It might have been the dust from the old curtains that caused it, but all of a sudden, Granger sneezed. Simultaneously, we heard something drop onto the floor above us. The three of us leapt together. "There's someone in the house!" Holly gasped.

Sure enough, to our horror, we heard someone cross the floor over our heads and slowly descend the stairs towards us. In an instant, we had dropped behind the couch under the window, clutching each other. I felt the prickle of fear on my scalp as the beam from a flashlight circled the room. In that brief moment I saw that the drawers in the buffet to my right had been pulled out, their contents spilled onto the floor, the cabinet doors yawning wide. The room had been ransacked!

Whoever it was moved on down the hall, opened one door after the other, fanning the light around each room before moving on to the next. It had to be Govier! He'd already been in the house when we arrived. Here we were hoping to trap him, and instead we were the ones who were trapped.

Praying Granger wouldn't throw up on the spot, I waited, feeling the sweat in the hands of the other two. We were well hidden, unless the man came back and decided to look behind the furniture. We heard him come down the hall again, pause for a few moments, and then the creak of the stairs as he went back up.

"Someone's got to go for help," I whispered, after a minute had passed. "Before he comes back down. Or gets away."

"Is it Govier, you think?" asked Holly.

I nodded. "I'm pretty sure. Either that or

another thief. He's already searched this room. Look over here." I indicated the opened drawers and cabinets.

"I'll go," said Granger, out of the blue.

"You will?"

"Just tell me what to do when I get there."

"Go wake up Sam Deitz," I said. "Tell him to call the police!"

"Right." Granger stood up, and Holly immediately yanked him back down again behind the couch. "And be quiet!" she ordered.

"You're pinching me," whined Granger.

"Sorry," Holly whispered, "but you've got to get out as quietly as we came in."

"And remember," I warned, solemnly handing him the flashlight, "you're leaving us in here, with him upstairs. He's already thought he heard something."

"I swear, guys." Granger's face was pale as death.

We watched him slip like a shadow across the room and down the hall. Holly and I held our breaths, listening as Granger, true to his word, made his escape without a sound.

Fourteen

Crouched together in our hiding place, Holly and I listened in fear. From the floor above us came the scrape of drawers opening, the sound of someone cursing, the creak of the floorboards. Holly's fingernails dug into my arm.

"It's okay," I promised, although I was not feeling as brave as I sounded. "Help is coming."

After about five minutes, while we still trembled behind the couch hardly daring to breathe, we heard the man coming back down the stairs. He turned when he reached the bottom, walked down the hall away from the living room and entered the kitchen.

He can't be leaving, I thought! Not till the police get here. But where were they? It was taking too long. And where was Granger? I began to wonder if he'd gone home and was hiding under the bed. I should have gone for help myself. Better yet, all three of us should have gotten out while we could.

"He's leaving!" Holly hissed against my ear.

"We can't let him," I croaked, and then, with the sensation that it was someone else I was watching, I raced down the hall to the kitchen. Holly was right behind.

"Get him!" I yelled, just as the man reached for the knob on the cellar door. He whirled around, saw us and slammed the door into us, catching us both behind it. The intruder pushed against it with all his weight, and I heard wood splintering, felt tremendous pressure against my body.

In the instant it took us to recover and burst out from behind the door, our assailant had plunged down the stairs and across the cellar to the outside door. Flinging it open, he darted up the steps, and there, blocking his exit with his wheelchair, was Mr. Samuel Deitz.

"Good evening, Victor," drawled Sam. "You're looking very well. For a dead man."

"Deitz!" Govier hesitated in the stairwell, but only for a second. "We'll see who's the dead man!" With a roar, he lunged for the top step, shoving the wheelchair away from him. The wheels caught in the edge of the brick path and the whole thing tipped sideways, toppling Deitz onto the ground at Granger's feet.

"Oh, no, you don't!" cried Granger, and Holly and I tackled Govier from behind, catching his pant legs just as he tried to leap away from the stairwell. The man fought us off and was scrambling on all fours when Granger launched a flying tackle from one side, giving the two of us time to jump him again. This time, Govier slammed hard into the ground, and the air in his lungs burst from him with a loud explosion.

A second later, a police car careened into the driveway. There was a brief wail from its siren, and another car swung in behind. Govier had regained his wind and kicked free of us again, struggling to his feet.

"Freeze!" roared a policeman.

It was all over for Victor Govier.

It took the three of us and one of the officers to haul Mr. Deitz back into his chair. He was dusty and dishevelled but not hurt. As he brushed the dust off the sleeves of his black jacket, his smile was triumphant. Victor Govier was led away in handcuffs.

*　　*　　*

"How much of that was true and how much just a pack of your usual lies?" Susan demanded, waylaying me on the front porch the next afternoon. Holly, Granger and I had been invited over to Sam Deitz's to await the return of Cyril Jones from hospital. Mr. D. wanted all four of us there to recount for Cyril the story of Victor Govier's capture.

Susan had laid the book she had been reading on the railing and was waiting for me to defend myself.

"It's all true," I said. "Everything you heard me tell Mom and Dad. That is just the way it happened."

She looked skeptical. "All that stuff about finding super-human strength?"

"That's just how it was," I insisted. "How else could three kids overpower a man who used to play college football?"

"Well, you can't blame me for asking." Susan picked up her book again. "Everyone knows how much you exaggerate."

"How much I *used to* exaggerate," I reminded her. "If you don't believe me, just ask Granger or Holly or Mr. Deitz."

The man in question was, as usual, out on his porch. He seemed none the worse for his tumble the night before. Now, he turned his head slowly in our direction. "You may take my word for it," Sam Deitz said solemnly. I saw the colour rise in Susan's cheeks, and she quickly lowered her eyes to her book again.

Climbing the steps to the porch next door, I dropped into one of the wicker chairs assembled there, to wait for the others. "Susan never believes me," I explained, ruefully. "I guess it's my own fault."

"And why is that?" asked Mr. Deitz.

"Oh, I always thought I had to make the truth a little more interesting. So I made up stories. Problem is, now people don't know when to believe me."

"Ah," the man nodded as if he understood, "you have a reputation to live down, in other words."

"I guess."

Mr. Deitz set the cigarette he'd been holding into an ashtray on his lap. "So, Martin, you're a teller of tall tales, are you?" He smiled at me. "That's fine, in its place, you know. It's when you confuse those tales with the truth that the trouble begins."

"Holly says my vivid imagination is one of my strengths," I pointed out.

"That's a more positive way to look at it," agreed Sam, with a slight nod. "You could use that imagination to your advantage, write wonderful fiction." He lifted his hands and flexed his fingers. "And now that Victor Govier is to get his just desserts, I hope to get back to my own writing."

"I'd heard you were a writer," I said. The truth was I'd never seen him do anything except watch the house across the road. "What do you write?"

"Sports stories, mostly."

"No kidding? So that's what you were doing when Victor Govier disappeared?"

Deitz nodded. "Victor and I met when we played

football at university. Later, we set up a business together, but Victor ran it, and I financed it from Montreal where I lived." He stubbed out the smouldering cigarette and set the ashtray on a small table beside him. "I really must do something about this disgusting habit," he muttered.

"My Mom can probably help you get rid of it," I offered, since he was the one who had mentioned it.

Deitz nodded grimly. "Cyril's sister is going to try a herbal remedy on me first," he said. "Oh, look now." Holly and Granger were crossing the lawn towards us. "Here come Mr. Fletcher and Ms. Valentine."

"Hey, what happened to you, Martin?" Granger grumbled as he trudged up the steps. "Thought we were supposed to meet in the deep end."

"Sorry," I acknowledged. "I was on my way over when I got into a discussion with Susan, and I forgot."

A few minutes later, Cyril Jones, wearing a rigid cervical collar, got out of a taxi at the curb. He used the ramp at the side rather than the stairs to reach the porch, walking with a stiff-legged gait. "I'm fine, I'm fine," he insisted when Mr. Deitz asked him repeatedly about how comfortable he was. "Just tell me what happened, how you managed to catch the thief."

"The very reason these youngsters are here,"

Deitz assured him, beaming. "As I told you on the telephone."

I couldn't help noticing that Susan, over at our house, was all ears while we recounted for Cyril the tale of our adventure the previous night. I was glad that she was listening. We had heard all the lectures from our parents, the police and Sam Deitz himself about how our escapade had been stupid and foolhardy. But we knew everyone was proud of us.

When we stopped for breath, Sam Deitz smiled warmly at Granger. "This, Cyril, is the brave lad who came to fetch me. He got me to the scene just in the nick of time. Why, the look on Victor's face was worth its weight in gold. I'm sorry you missed it."

"I didn't exactly get you there, Mr. Deitz," Granger blushed. "You were halfway across the street before I could tell you what was happening."

"Well, I had fallen asleep," Deitz admitted. "That was unforgivable!"

"You really are a hero, Grange," I said. "The way you got out of that house so quietly."

"And did you notice?" Holly added. "You didn't throw up!"

"Hey, that's right," grinned Granger. "Well, that's a first. I guess I really am a hero."

"I'd say you're all heroes," declared Mr. Deitz. Then, throwing back his head, he gave a hearty laugh, the first time I'd heard the sound. "What was it you said, Mr. Fletcher, when you came to fetch me? That 'something big was going down'?"

"Well, it was!" Granger declared. The look on his face was one of pure joy.

Victor Govier's capture was reason to celebrate, and Sam Deitz insisted that he was going to get everyone some refreshment. When it turned out that the drink we were being offered was carrot juice, the Deep End Gang decided we had pressing business elsewhere.

Before we said goodbye, we were assured that Cyril Jones would resume his duties gradually, as his strength returned. Cyril's sister, the herbologist who lived on the next block, had offered him a place to stay until he was able to get another car and return to his own apartment across town. It was her garage he'd used to hide the Corvette, while he maintained his nightly surveillance inside the Govier house.

*　　*　　*

A few minutes later, the Deep End Gang was back in the chairs in the old swimming pool. It was going to take a while for us to wipe the satisfied grins off our faces, but already Granger was wondering what our next mission would be.

It looked as if our regular meeting place had

been given another reprieve: Holly's father had decided that his number one priority before summer was over was to build his wife a gazebo.

At the speed that Mr. Valentine is moving with his projects, I may not even get a chance to swim in Holly's pool before it's time to move again. Lately though, Mom and Dad have both been talking about Branch, Ontario, being a pretty nice place to put down roots.

I could handle that.

Acknowledgments
I would like to thank my friend Janet Lunn for suggesting I tell this story, my niece Beth Bonvie for bringing me up to date on life in a military family, and my nephew Paul Hobson, who owned the '86 Corvette.

Peggy Dymond Leavey was born in Toronto, one of a family of five children. Her father was in the Canadian military and, as a result of his frequent postings, she received her education in nine different schools between Winnipeg and Fort Chambly, Quebec.

The mother of three grown children, Peggy now lives in the Trenton area of Ontario with her husband and their Labrador retriever, Belle. Her third book for Napoleon, *Sky Lake Summer*, was published in 1999 and was nominated for the Silver Birch Award and the Manitoba Young Readers' Choice Award. She is also the author of *Help Wanted: Wednesdays Only*, *A Circle in Time* and *Finding My Own Way*.